P9-CFI-661

THE
DOCTOR'S
WIFE

New

HUR   Hurst, Daniel
           DISCARD
           The doctor's wife

                              8/2023

BOOKS BY DANIEL HURST

Til Death Do Us Part

The Passenger

The Woman at the Door

He Was a Liar

The Wrong Woman

We Used to Live Here

The Couple at Table Six

We Tell No One

The Accident

What My Family Saw

The Intruder

The Couple in the Cabin

THE
DOCTOR'S
WIFE

DANIEL HURST

bookouture

Published by Bookouture in 2023

An imprint of Storyfire Ltd.
Carmelite House
50 Victoria Embankment
London EC4Y 0DZ

www.bookouture.com

Copyright © Daniel Hurst, 2023

Daniel Hurst has asserted his right to be identified as the author of this work.

All rights reserved. No part of this publication may be reproduced, stored in any retrieval system, or transmitted, in any form or by any means, electronic, mechanical, photocopying, recording or otherwise, without the prior written permission of the publishers.

ISBN: 978-1-0314-941-7
eBook ISBN: 978-1-80314-940-0

This book is a work of fiction. Names, characters, businesses, organizations, places and events other than those clearly in the public domain, are either the product of the author's imagination or are used fictitiously. Any resemblance to actual persons, living or dead, events or locales is entirely coincidental.

PROLOGUE

As the woman at the window watched the activity on the beach, she knew the body on the sand was going to be the event that turned this quiet seaside village into a hive of activity for several days to come. This isolated place was usually only frequented by local residents, delivery drivers from the nearby towns and the occasional tourist passing in and out of Scotland. Now it would be teeming with forensic experts, journalists and bystanders harbouring a morbid curiosity.

That was the thing about the appearance of a body in an unexpected place.

It demanded attention.

And it always got it.

That was never more evident than on the day that the body of Drew Devlin was discovered sprawled out on the stretch of sand that lined this picturesque piece of coastline in the North of England.

The wet, white T-shirt that clung to the twisted torso was the same colour as the cloud-filled sky above, and the temperature of the corpse was as cold as the weather in this rainswept, wind-battered part of the country. The black shorts covering the pale, lifeless thighs were almost as dark as the sky on the horizon, another storm incoming for a village that had already endured so much and had even more trying challenges to come. And one grey trainer on the left foot, slowly losing its pristine condition as specks of dirt and sand were flicked onto it by the rolling tide that washed against the body in a weary fashion, and what could be considered a disrespectful one too.

The shoe that should have been on the right foot was missing, but if anybody looked for it then they would surely see it bobbing around in the sea several feet away, like a ship without a sailor, drifting aimlessly, most likely to come back to land with a bump at some point but, for now, completely at the mercy of the ice-cold current.

But nobody was looking at the shoe. Everybody was looking at the person it belonged to and that included the woman at the window. She kept watching as the emergency services came to carry out their grim tasks, and she continued to watch as the sun began to set on this terrible day. That was because the body out there on the sand was of a man that she had once loved. But she hadn't been the only one in this village who had loved the deceased. He was popular with the opposite sex, too popular, if anything.

And that was one of the reasons why he was now dead.

TWO WEEKS EARLIER

ONE

FERN

As the car I'm a passenger in comes to a stop on the sweeping driveway of my idyllic new home, a million thoughts are running through my mind. For me, the day an adult moves to a new house is not too dissimilar to the day a child starts at a new school. There's an air of nervousness that accompanies the worry of whether the right thing is being done. There is the dull ache of anxiety in the pit of the stomach caused by the regret of leaving old friends behind and the possibility that new friends might be harder to come by in this fresh setting. And, most of all, there is the unmistakable realisation that no matter what happens next, life is never going to be the same again.

How could I describe this new place? For starters, I'd say it's very different to the house I'm moving from, although that's not necessarily a bad thing. I mean, who can ever complain about upsizing, right? But there's more to life than size, as any woman likes to remind a man, so I have always been smart enough to look beyond that and get into the details.

Technically, this property is a beautiful structure, a two-floor whitewashed building consisting of four bedrooms, two bathrooms, a kitchen I once only dreamed about and the type of dining room that would be perfect for entertaining guests. That's before even mentioning the spacious lounge area and the gorgeous back garden that seems to go on forever. But as good as all that is, it's more about what's at the front of the location of the house, which is even more stunning than what's inside or behind it. That's because the property couldn't be located in a more idyllic spot. Built just across the road from sand and water, the house overlooks the Solway Firth, a stretch of water between England and Scotland that forms part of the border between the two nations. And what a pretty border it is. On a day with fine weather, much like today, and the previous day I came here to inspect the property, the views are incredible, you can see for miles both along the water's edge and also straight across, meaning a person can be standing in one country but looking at another.

It's incredible to be able to see Scotland on a clear day, or 'The Bonnie Banks' as it has been referred to in the past by many a person. That might sound all well and good, but this is the UK, so what's it like on a bad-weather day? Fortunately, I've not been here to experience one of those yet, but I can safely assume this place has a very different feel to it when the sun is obscured, the clouds have wrapped themselves around the land-scape, and the grains of sand on the beach are being peppered with ice-cold raindrops from the heavens.

But it's not the prospect of inclement weather that is giving me cause for concern about moving here, nor is it the property itself, because it really is a stunning place and one anybody would be lucky to call their own. No, there is one other reason why I have my reservations about what I am doing as I sit in my car and think about the new future I have agreed to be a part of, and the simplest way of describing my state of mind at the moment is this:

Conflicted.

Ask around, and I'm sure there are plenty of people I've

known over the years who would be happy to describe me. But if I had to describe myself then I'd sum myself up in three words.

A city girl.

That's right, I love a concrete jungle. The high-rise buildings. The coffee shops on every corner. The bars and restaurants that stay open late and the cafes that open early. The shopping centres and the parks. The intimate theatres and the cavernous arenas. The choice of supermarkets and the array of transport links. And the people, oh so many people. Commuters. Students. Retailers. Baristas. Waiters. Street performers. Joggers. Dogwalkers. All hustling and bustling with places to go and people to see. Bumping elbows with one another on the train or just standing behind each other in the line to get a mocha.

Energy. Vibrancy. *Life.*

I've always lived in a city. Manchester mainly, as that's where I grew up and have spent most of my adult life, only broken up by a three-year spell at York University and a two-year work placement in the biggest English city of all, London. Those experiences mean I have never known anything other than 24/7 noise and action and funny smells and the chance to find somewhere open to enjoy a drink, whether it's 3 p.m. or 3 a.m., and while some people might hate it, I bloody love it.

As far as I'm concerned, a city isn't just a big collection of buildings, it's actually a living, breathing organism made up of the people who call it home, and I have always been one of those people.

Until today.

Now I am no longer a city dweller. Rather, I am somebody who has to find comfort in open spaces, long silences and, most of all, solitude. From a population of over two million to barely five hundred, and I'm pretty sure that is counting the sheep in the nearby hills too.

So long, Manchester.

Hello, Arberness.

Of the people who live in this village, I'm told that the majority are those whose relatives had lived here before them. There have been several generations of the same family around here, and not many of them left the village for bigger and busier pastures, instead staying because they took pride in their remote region and saw the beauty in being somewhere less overrun than the cities and towns nearby. But a few residents were not born here nor had they any previous connection to the village before they settled in it. Instead, they are simply people shunning the major metropolitan hubs and seeking the quiet life as they grow older in a place where there is certainly plenty of quiet.

There's no doubt about it.

This is going to take some getting used to.

'I guess we should get out and give the removal guys some help.'

The voice of the man sitting beside me in the car snaps me out of my trance, and when I turn to look at him, I see that he is smiling at me. It's a nice smile. A handsome one. The same one that charmed me all those years ago, when I first saw it flashed in my direction, and the same smile I saw as I made my way down the aisle in my white dress. His smile was wide then, and it's certainly wide now, but I've never seen it bigger than on the day six months ago when I agreed to leave our old life behind and move here, to this remote place, to start again with the man that I married.

Yep, this move was my husband's idea. I'll make that clear now, just in case everything goes wrong soon, which is a very real possibility. That's right, moving out here to the middle of nowhere was the thought and suggestion of Drew Devlin, or Doctor Drew Devlin, as he likes to introduce himself to others.

'I didn't spend all those years at medical school just to be another Drew,' he told me once as we were on our way home from a dinner party, and after I'd asked him why he insisted on giving his professional title outside of the workplace. 'It's important to include that little extra word at the beginning of my name. I worked hard for it and, if nothing else, it's a conversation starter.'

I hadn't bothered to challenge him on that, although I did tease him a little about it just for fun. I also made sure to tell him that it didn't matter to me whether he was Doctor Drew, Dentist Drew or even just Dreary Drew because he was my man, and I was proud of him whatever he did for work.

But while I didn't often mention to my husband how much I liked the fact that he was a fully qualified and practising doctor, because his ego certainly didn't need another boost, the truth is that I love what he does for a living. It's a well-respected and very important profession, not to mention well paid, as well as being very convenient whenever I have any symptoms that I might need a quick opinion on.

There's never a need for me to wait for an appointment when I can just lift up my T-shirt and ask the man in bed beside me if my new mole looks like it might be trouble. It might not be my sexiest move but when you're pushing forty, as I am, being sexy is way down on the To-Do List.

But it's not all fun being a doctor's wife. That's because a job in the medical profession demands dedication, diligence and, most of all, a willingness to work long hours to see all the patients who have illnesses and ailments that require special care and attention. It's simply not possible for a doctor to do a half-hearted job. It's all or nothing, give great care or no care at all. And Doctor Drew always prides himself on giving the best care to his patients that he can. The problem was, he had just too many of those pesky patients, hence the idea to move out of the city and continue his career somewhere a little quieter.

'Imagine it. With less patients to see every day, I can finish at five o'clock, or maybe even earlier,' Drew had told me when he was pitching me the idea. 'Isn't that what you've always wanted? More time together? Well, it's never going to happen here. But if we move, it can be a reality.'

I remember the expression on his face when he had said those words to me, or rather I remember his piercing blue eyes staring into my own and making me feel like they always did, which was special. He has always had that power over me, like I imagine all good-looking men have over women, in that one look could usually melt a heart and get him what he wanted. The fact he always has such relaxed body language helps him too. He's never stiff or unsure. He always acts as if he is fully confident about what he is saying and, I guess, for the most part he is.

'You know I want you to finish work earlier,' I'd agreed, much preferring having my husband home at a decent hour as opposed to him walking through the front door at seven or eight o'clock, grumbling about a backlog of referral letters and an overcrowded waiting room. 'But it's a bit extreme to go from here to there, isn't it? I mean, we have everything we could ever need here. Family, friends, all our favourite places. What would we have there?'

'Oh, I don't know. How about peace? Tranquillity. Fresh air. Miles of open space to relax in. Long walks on the beach. Village fetes. An actual community to be a part of rather than just being another statistic squashed into an overpopulated section of the country. And, most importantly, for the first time in my life, and our marriage, a proper work/life balance.'

I had to give it to Drew. He did make a compelling argument for why we should consider moving. But it was an argument that he would have to sharpen and refine over several days before I eventually started to come around to his way of thinking.

'I can see you're really serious about this,' I had told him one night after he had come home grumpy again from another tiring day. 'You know I have my concerns about it. But if it's really what you want then I'll do it. I'll agree to move. But on one condition. We find the perfect house. If I'm going to be in the middle of nowhere surrounded by nothing but bleating sheep and crazy village folk, I at least want a nice kitchen. You promised me a breakfast bar when we were engaged, and I'm yet to see any evidence of one.'

That breakfast bar was just one of many grand ambitions I had harboured ever since I got into a serious relationship with Drew. We'd often lie in bed together for hours in the early days of our romance and discuss all sorts of dreams, some sensible, some a little crazier. Places we wanted to visit. Cars we wanted to drive. What we wanted to be doing when we reach retirement age. I'm pleased to say that many of those dreams came true. But, as always in life, some fell by the wayside.

I've never seen Drew so happy as the night I agreed that we would leave Manchester and move to Arberness, a place he picked, he told me, because he had been there a couple of times while coming back from lads' trips to Scotland, and it had always captured his imagination. I was yet to be as convinced as he was that the tiny village was the best place for us to begin the next chapter of our lives, but once I'd agreed the moving plans began in earnest. Our house went on the market for a very profitable price while we quickly set about finding a new home in the village. It only took a couple of trips up north before we found the house we wanted.

'It's perfect,' Drew had told me before I had even laid eyes on it, but once I had, I felt the same way. As anyone in a marriage will know, agreeing on something is half the battle, but this was one thing we didn't have an argument on. The house was perfect. The size, the location, the price. It ticked every box we had when we first made contact with an estate agent. And here we are now, with the removal men carrying our boxes into it.

And so, as Drew and I get out of our car, it is now official. We live here now. Not back there in the city, where everything is familiar and accessible, but here, where everything is new, spread out and smells strange, as if my nostrils can't quite understand why the air is clean and not filled with exhaust fumes.

Have I done the right thing, or have I made a mistake? Am I going to like it here or grow to resent it? Will I make new friends, or will my only company during the working week be whatever sheep wanders up to the wall at the bottom of our garden? And will I fall in love with the view of the beach at the front of my house, or will its sands start to torment me over time, causing me to long for the familiar feeling of the hard concrete of the city streets that I once walked on with such confidence?

I suppose only time will tell. But as we go inside our new house and think about making a start on unpacking all the boxes that are beginning to pile up in our hallway, I know one thing is for sure.

My husband is very, very happy to be here.

Possibly a little *too* happy.

TWO

DREW

I did it. What seemed like an impossible task has now been achieved. I persuaded my wife to leave behind the city that she loves and accompany me here, and now that we have officially made the move, everything is still on track. I'm so giddy I could do a little dance, but that is not quite appropriate, plus I don't want to embarrass myself in front of the removal guys who are just leaving, so I keep a lid on my excitement for now. I really am happy, and it has nothing at all to do with this new house. It's simply because I've got my own way.

Fern believes me.

She thinks I suggested this because I'm seeking the quiet life.

If only she knew the truth.

'Can you take that upstairs, please?' my wife asks me as she points to a very heavy-looking cardboard box with the words 'master bedroom' scrawled across it in black marker pen. 'I guess the removal guys didn't take the time to read the notes I made for them and check which room these boxes were supposed to go in.'

'It's my fault. I should have monitored them more,' I say

before letting out a weary groan as I lift the box and head for the stairs.

'I guess they got distracted with all the football talk,' Fern replies with a wry smile, referring to how I got into such a deep conversation about the current state of Manchester United with the removals men that they ended up having to hurry to finish on time.

'I was just being friendly. I imagine they welcome a distraction in their line of work. Not everyone loves their job like I do.'

I'm exaggerating a little about how much I adore my profession as I climb the stairs, but there is some truth in it. I once took great pride in being a doctor, following in the footsteps of my father who pretended like he would have been happy for me to do anything career-wise, but clearly harboured hopes that I would follow him into the medical profession. I had my doubts but armed with the requisite intellect to not only study medicine but pass all the exams and tests along the way, I found myself warming to the idea of being a GP. It was a proud day when I became fully qualified, more for my parents than for me, and I have tried to retain that sense of pride throughout my career, although the fantasy of the job differs somewhat from the reality of it. It seems less about helping to save lives and more about managing bureaucracy now, definitely more than it was in my father's day, but I don't want too many people to know that. That's because I like the respect and admiration I get from others when they find out what I do for a living, and it'll only be tainted if they discover that most of my day is spent pushing paper at my desk.

Or at least it used to be anyway.

But here in Arberness, I'll have fewer patients, which means I can give a better quality of care. I might also get five minutes in between individual consultations to have a breather as well, which will be a big bonus. Gone are the days when I couldn't even go to the toilet or eat a sandwich without feeling like I was adding another delay to an already severely bogged down system. Things should be sleeker here, more manageable and, ultimately, easier than they were in Manchester. That place was stressful on a good day and downright overwhelming on a bad one due to the sheer bulk of the workload thrust upon me.

I put down the heavy box in the master bedroom, alongside all the other ones that made it up here earlier, and a quick examination of the room highlights just how much work Fern and I have ahead of ourselves before we get this place looking like we want it to. Right now, it looks more like a warehouse than a home, but we'll get there, or at least my wife will. I'm due to start work tomorrow, which means I won't be around to help out here as much as I could do, but I know Fern will manage it. Besides, it'll keep her occupied and reduce the chances of her getting bored, then lonely, then asking for us to move back to Manchester. The busier she is, the less likely it is she will find out what I am really here for.

I should go back downstairs and help move the next box, but, before I do, I walk over to the window and gaze out across the water that now forms what will be the first thing we see every day when we open the curtains. While taking in the beauty of the area, I think about the real reason I made us move here, and as lovely as the scenery is, it has nothing to do with that at all.

Instead, it has everything to do with Alice.

I let out a deep sigh as I think about the one woman I truly love, the woman I am not married to but who has got such a place in my heart that I have been willing to uproot my life and start again up here, in what is essentially the middle of nowhere. I think about where she might be now, and know that wherever she is, it can't be far from where I am. That's because Alice lives in this village, too, and considering how small it is I'll never be more than a couple of streets away from her at any one time.

That thought warms my bones, and I'm sure I'll need that warmth during these colder months as the temperature plunges and causes this place to feel a little less tranquil and a lot more testing.

My eyes stay on the water as I think about Alice and how good it will be to be with her again. It's been six long months since I've seen her beautiful face, and I've spent all that time recapping the final conversation we had. It was the one in which she told me that our affair was over. To prove it, she was moving away from Manchester and starting again with her husband, Rory, who had no idea his wife had been unfaithful to him. Just like my wife had no idea I'd done the same to her.

To say I was devasted at Alice's decision would be an understatement. Of course, I knew what we were doing was wrong, seeing each other behind our respective partner's backs and all, but it wasn't just some casual fling that was purely about sex. No, our relationship ran much deeper than that. I fell in love with Alice during the course of our affair and, despite what she said the last time we spoke, I know that she fell in love with me too.

Our affair started a year ago on what had been an otherwise average and mundane day in my life as a city-centre GP. After spending twelve long hours handing out prescriptions for painkillers and convincing most of the patients that the mild symptoms they were reporting to me didn't mean they were, in fact, dying, I'd been in need of a strong drink. That's why I'd called into the pub just around the corner from my workplace, so I could grab a beer before heading home and telling my wife, Fern, all about my day. But my life was to change forever, not long after I had ordered that beer, because no sooner had I taken my seat at the bar and given the nod to the barman to pour me a pint, than I noticed her.

The long blonde hair. The shapely curves. And the smile that made me feel like I was a teenager again. I had no idea who the pretty woman in the pub was because I'd never seen her around that part of the city before.

But oh, how I wished I had.

I wished she was one of my patients and came to see me every week, even if there was nothing wrong with her. Doctors hate hypochondriacs, but I'd have given anything to have had her as my number one patient, knocking on my door every day with some new report of a false illness that she might have. Anything to be near her. To talk to her. To find out more.

I knew the chances of a woman like her stumbling into my surgery were slim and not just because she looked positively healthy. It was because, quite simply, I wasn't that lucky. Only incredibly good fortune could allow me to cross paths with someone like *her* and, while I had a good life in terms of being married, having a stable career and enough family and friends around me to never feel lonely, I knew meeting *her* would somehow top it all.

I had sat and watched her from across the pub as she chatted with a female friend at a table over in the corner, but I barely tasted my beer as I sipped it because I was so lost in fantasising about my new discovery.

What was her name? Where did she live? What did she do for work?

And most importantly of all, would she be interested in talking to me?

The sight of the small diamond ring on her left hand didn't put me off at all because I had my own wedding ring on too. But, at that moment, I hadn't been thinking about any potential affair and certainly not about how getting involved with her could cause my life to change in all sorts of unpredictable ways. I'd simply wanted her to notice me. To see me. To admire me like I was admiring her.

I had no choice but to order another beer as I had sat and waited in that pub for the pretty woman in the corner to potentially come nearer, and eventually my patience paid off. With the venue having grown busier around us, she had approached the bar to get another round of drinks and, once she was closer to me, I didn't miss my chance.

I complimented her on her appearance, cutting straight to the chase because I didn't have time to waste, nor did I want to be like every other man in the place who was simply looking at her but not doing anything about it. She accepted the compliment before returning it by telling me that she liked my suit and then asking if I worked in an office.

As always, I jumped at the chance to tell her that I was a doctor. I saw that my profession impressed her, based on the look in her eyes as I spoke. I made sure to show more of an interest in her by asking plenty of questions of my own and, pretty soon, ordering another drink was the last thing on her mind. After her friend joined us, presumably to find out why her drink was taking so long to materialise, she lied and told her I was an old acquaintance from university, and highlighted how unlikely it was for the two of us to have bumped into one another after all these years, but that was clearly just a ploy to get the friend to leave the two of us alone. Once the friend had departed, we stayed together in that pub until closing time, talking and flirting until it genuinely looked like we were old friends and not just two people who had only just met.

I didn't get a kiss from Alice that night, mainly because both of us knew the other one was taken, and we were still trying to do the right thing. But I did get her phone number and that was all I needed to keep in touch with her and set up future meetings, meetings that I was sure would eventually result in us being intimate.

And sure enough, they did.

All my late arrivals home were easy to dismiss with Fern: I just told her that work was crazy, and she believed it because work had always been that way for me. But rather than being stuck in my doctor's surgery drowning beneath a pile of prescriptions, I was checking in and out of city-centre hotels with Alice and feeling more alive than I had felt in years.

Obviously, I felt bad about what I was doing behind Fern's back, just like Alice felt bad about what she was doing to her partner, Rory. But we just couldn't help ourselves. Like a child finding themselves with the key to a sweet shop, we were making the most of the opportunity to do whatever we wanted. It was dangerous, and I knew I would break Fern's heart if she ever found out about it, but I was confident that would never happen. We'd kept it secret for long enough, so why couldn't we keep doing that forever?

The way I saw it, it wasn't mine or Alice's fault that we had met each other *after* we had already settled down. It was just life. Mad, unpredictable life. The main thing was that we had found each other, and as we were still only on the cusp of forty, I felt like we still had plenty of time to enjoy ourselves in secret.

And then Alice told me she was ending it and moving away.

I grit my teeth as I remain standing by the bedroom window, watching the water swilling and sloshing around in the bay. The hurt I felt when Alice told me that I was to leave her alone and never contact her again is still very much real, even if half a year has passed and she probably thinks I've forgotten about her now. But I haven't. I'm as madly in love with her as I was the first time I saw her in that pub, and that's why I've taken the rather extreme measure of moving here. Alice has no idea that I am going to come back into her life, but, when she realises what I have done, she will surely see that I am serious about us and give our love affair another go. It's just a shame an affair is all it can ever be. That's because we can never be together properly, not as an official couple. That would require me to leave Fern and, despite considering this as an option many times, I don't think it's a viable one. That's because Fern knows too many things about me.

Things I'm not proud of.

And things that could get me in serious trouble if they ever came out.

I don't see what I am doing as stalking. I see it as romantic. I hope Alice will see it the same way. As for Fern and Rory, they won't know what is going on, just like they had no idea before, and I'll keep it that way until Alice is back in my arms again. But there is a small chance Alice might not react well to my reappearance and, just in case, I'm not burning any bridges with my wife. Better to be a married man with a complicated love life than a divorced doctor whom everyone pities.

For now, I'll keep my little secret and see how all of this plays out.

What does life in this village have in store for me?

Well, just like in the city, I'm going to do everything I can to get exactly what I want.

THREE

FERN

The first person to visit us in our new home is Audrey, our elderly next-door neighbour, and she doesn't come empty-handed.

'I've made you a lasagne,' she says as I welcome her in with the hot dish she is carrying. 'I imagine all your pots and pans are still in boxes, so I thought you might need something quick for your dinner this evening. It won't take long to heat up. You do have a microwave, don't you?'

'Yes, of course. Thank you, that's very kind of you,' I tell her as she steps into my wide and well-lit hallway, and I lock the door behind her.

'Oh, you don't need to worry about locking your doors here, dear. There is no crime in Arberness.'

'Sorry, just a habit from living in the city,' I say, not sure why I'm apologising for locking my own front door, nor why I lied about it being more out of habit than anything else. The truth is I would always lock the door to my house no matter where I am, who I am with and what time of day it might be. A person can never be too careful, even in a low-crime area like this one.

'Ahh, so you've moved here from the city, have you?' Audrey says as I gratefully accept the dish from her and invite her to follow me into the kitchen. 'Well, I won't hold that against you.'

She lets me know she's only teasing, and I laugh, warming to her even more.

'So, what took you so long to come to your senses and move out to the country?'

'It was my idea actually.'

Drew appears then, popping up out of the dining room with another box in his hands and a big smile on his face. He never has any trouble charming people, and I suspect he's going to get straight to work charming our new neighbour. Sure enough, he does just that, putting the box down so he can shake Audrey's hand before he compliments her on her woolly sweater.

'Thank you. I knitted it myself.'

'A talented woman. You'll get on well with my wife then.'

I roll my eyes at him, wondering how he can somehow manage to flatter two people with one swift comment. I head into the kitchen and put the lasagne in the fridge before trying to find the kettle so I can make us all a cup of tea.

It's a pleasure to move around this spacious room, opening the oak cupboards to pull out cups and placing them down on stone countertops, the likes of which give this room a rustic feel, as well as make me believe they were crafted and installed by somebody who really has a passion and respect for both interior design as well as the historic area this house sits in.

'So which city is it that you have moved from?' Audrey asks me as she stands in the doorway while Drew goes upstairs with his box. I'm glad that at least one of us is still working on tidying this place up.

'Manchester.'

'Oh, I see. You're going to get on well with the Richardsons then. They're a couple of a similar age to you, and they moved here from Manchester last year.'

'Do you hear that, Drew?' I call out upstairs. 'We're not the only Mancunians in the village!'

'Thank God for that!' he calls back in jest, but he doesn't bother to come back down, so I guess I'm left to make all the conversation with Audrey. Thankfully, it's pretty painless because she's a chatty soul who has no problem filling in any silences before they can really form.

'Their names are Rory and Alice, and they are a lovely couple,' Audrey tells me, continuing on the topic of the other couple from Manchester who now call this village home. 'Rory has one of those fancy IT jobs where he gets to just work from home. Isn't that something? There was nothing like that in my day. Imagine being paid to sit around in your pyjamas. The world's gone mad if you ask me. But he must be doing well because Alice doesn't have to work.'

'Oh, that's nice,' I say, neglecting to mention that I am also married to a man with a job that pays well enough to mean I don't have to seek out employment either. I'm sure Audrey will ask me what I do at some point, but I'll wait until she does because I don't want it to seem like I am bragging. It would be hard not to make it sound like I was though, simply because getting to spend my time pursuing my hobbies of homemaking and catching up on episodes of slightly trashy reality television is clearly a much more fun way of living than answering to a boss in a stuffy office. I love that I have freedom in my day, even if it comes at the cost of not being around as many people as I used to do. But then again, who wants to be around boring Brenda in accounts or Bill, the weirdo by the photocopier? I did the 9–5 life for several years and, by the end of it, after too many nights of coming home stressed from banal deadlines and in tears after an awful commute, Drew said I didn't have to work any longer if it was making me unhappy.

I couldn't resign quick enough.

'But Alice keeps busy enough,' Audrey goes on. 'She volunteers at the local library as well as helps out at the weekly coffee morning at the village church hall. You should come to that, dear, unless you'll be working then. It's at 10 a.m. every Wednesday morning, and there's twelve of us that attend regularly. It's a good chance to get together and have a bit of a gossip, especially for some of us older folks who live alone now.'

I tell Audrey that I will be sure to be at the next coffee morning before taking the hint about Audrey being by herself and asking about her background a little more. It turns out that she was married for over fifty years before her partner, Reg, passed away, although she seems chipper enough to not let it get her down too much on a day-to-day basis.

'We had a wonderful relationship,' Audrey assures me. 'It was truly a blessing to be together for so many years. It's lovely to see a younger couple moving to the village who seem to be just as happy as me and my Reg were.'

I smile at her suggestion that Drew and I are happy, pleased that she has assumed that from only two minutes in our company, before I eventually find the kettle and go about making us that cup of tea.

I spend the next hour listening to Audrey give me a crash course on village life, hearing handy hints on all sorts of things from which shop to go to if I want a good block of cheese to which date market day falls on and how to get the most of that. It's all very helpful stuff, although listening to it all isn't helping me get any further ahead with the unpacking, so it's a relief when Audrey eventually finishes her drink and tells me she will get out of our way so we can get back to work.

I thank her for calling around as she exits the house, and she reminds me about the weekly coffee morning one more time before she departs until, eventually, I can close and re-lock the door again. Then I return to the kitchen, glancing out of the window at the view of the rolling hills behind our spacious, if a little unkept, back garden, before I start emptying another box of plates. As I do, I think about how lovely it was to have a neighbour call by. It certainly differs from the experience Drew and I had when we bought a house in Manchester, because nobody on the street came to welcome us then.

That's just one of the many differences between being in a city and being in a village like this one, I think as I put the plates in their new home in the cupboard above the sink. But five minutes have barely passed before I change my mind and put the plates into a different cupboard, before giving it a little more thought and deciding they were actually better in the first place after all.

This is going to take me longer than I thought.

If Drew was in the room now, he would lament my OCD tendencies and just tell me to make a decision and stick with it, but I'm not like him. I have to think everything through carefully, and even then I'm prone to changing my mind and making a new plan. Not like him. He seems to breeze through life and happily watch everything fall into place. But I have to work harder at it. Nothing comes as naturally to me as it does to Drew. I wonder if that's why we ended up together. Opposites attract, as they say. Well, we are certainly different, him and I, and I get further proof of that when I go upstairs to see how he is getting on with the unpacking, only to find that he is sitting on one of the boxes staring at something on his phone.

'What are you doing? We don't have time for this,' I say as I try to sneak a peek at his screen, but he swipes his device away before I can get a good look at it.

'Sorry, just checking the football news,' Drew tells me sheepishly before stuffing his device back into his pocket and yawning awkwardly.

'I really thought you'd be further ahead than this. You've

been up here by yourself for an hour. Don't tell me you've been on your phone that whole time.'

'No, of course not. I've been unpacking... a little. I got bored. And, besides, you've been chatting with the neighbour for all this time, so you can hardly call me lazy.'

'I didn't say lazy. I was just thinking it.'

Drew tickles me for teasing him, and my loud screaming fills the silence of this cavernous home before he eventually stops and allows me to get my breath back. I lost count of how many times he did the same thing to me when we first fell in love, his delicate hands on my body, locating my most ticklish parts and causing me to laugh uncontrollably. I guess you could say I was putty in his hands and, boy, did he know it. That was probably one of the reasons he was always grinning when he was around me. He knew I was enamoured with him. And that smile of his only deepened the spell I was under.

'Stop it. We don't have time for games. We've got so much to do. We need to make a start on building the bed.'

'Oh, really. What do you have in mind?'

'Sleep.'

I laugh at my husband's disappointed face before telling him to go and get his toolbox so we can get going on the building work.

'Yeah, we could build the bed. Or, I was thinking, how about we leave all the jobs for the time being and go out and explore our new surroundings? The pub should be open by now. We could go for a drink. It might be a good chance to go and meet a few more of the locals?'

I want to tell him that we definitely don't have time for that, but I am feeling mightily overwhelmed by the size of the tasks surrounding me in this house, so a drink might not be such a bad idea after all.

'Okay, let's go. But just for one,' I tell him, and he looks as happy as a kid on Christmas morning as he heads for the stairs.

What is it with men and pubs?

They really don't need much to be happy, do they?

At least my husband is predictable, if nothing else.

FOUR

DREW

I'm striding quickly into the heart of the village with Fern by my side, pleased that she agreed to make a trip to the pub and optimistic about who we might see along the way. I'm aware that Alice could be around any corner, this is the village she told me she was moving to, after all, and I'm keeping a lookout for her as we walk along the quiet streets, but as the pub comes into sight, I still haven't spotted her yet. But no worries. The day is still young.

'Slow down a bit. What's the rush?' Fern says, and it's only then I realise that she has fallen a few steps behind me. 'You can't be that desperate for a beer, can you?'

'Sorry,' I say, easing the pace a little, but only a little because it's hard to contain the mixture of frustration and excitement that is building up in my body at the moment.

The excitement stems from wondering if this will be the first time I see Alice in half a year, while the frustration comes from my oblivious wife having no idea what really makes me happy in this world. She thinks all I'm bothered about is having a drink, and while that's convenient enough for me to keep my secrets hidden, it does irritate me a little that she thinks I'm so basic.

To her, I'm just a guy who prefers the pub over housework, which makes me pretty ordinary. In reality, I am someone who is seeking real adventure and passion in my life, and that means I'm infinitely more interesting than she actually realises. I guess she has a blind spot when it comes to me, and that probably explains why I grew bored of her and found solace in the arms of another woman. I'm not sure Fern has ever really understood me.

Alice gets me.

And, pretty soon, she is going to know I'm back.

The thought had crossed my mind that perhaps I should message Alice to let her know that I was in the village and wanted to see her. I figured doing that would give her a chance to process it rather than be shocked, but, in the end, I couldn't pluck up the courage to do it. I sat with my phone in my hand for almost an hour while Fern was downstairs with Audrey, contemplating whether or not to reach out to Alice, and I spent so long pondering it that Fern almost caught me with my other woman's contact details on my screen. But, as always, I kept the truth hidden and pretended I was just looking at the football news before putting my phone quickly back in my pocket, where it has stayed ever since.

I'm not going to message Alice because I'd prefer to just meet her organically somewhere around the village. And when I do, I'll be able to see what her natural reaction is to my presence without her having the chance to cover it up. I know she'll be surprised, to say the least, and I'm sure she'll try and have a quiet word with me and tell me that I shouldn't have come here. But none of that will matter if I see what I am hoping to see, which is that spark in her eyes that she had the first time she saw me in that pub. If I see it then, despite whatever misgivings she might have, I'll know I'm still in with a chance of rekindling our relationship.

'The King's Head,' I say as I see the sign for the pub up ahead. 'Why are so many pubs named after the body parts of royalty?'

'It's just a name,' Fern replies, slightly out of breath from our brisk walk to get here, and even that annoys me. *Alice is much fitter than you,* I can't help thinking. *Maybe that's another reason she took your place in my heart.*

'I suppose,' I reply as I turn my head and look into a shop window, wondering if Alice could be on the other side of the glass. But there's no one in there other than an elderly man standing behind a counter, and he just nods at me as I pass him, acknowledging me in his modest, masculine way. I nod back, disappointed but focused on the next place of interest, which is a post office, but again, a quick glance through the window there does not reveal Alice either.

The rather sudden and perhaps paranoid thought that I have timed my arrival in this village with Alice being away on some kind of holiday hits me then. What if she's abroad, sunning herself on a beach somewhere? I'd have to wait for her to get back and when might that be? I've waited long enough to see her. I can't face waiting another hour, let alone another day.

We make it all the way to the pub, and I'm sweating a little, though it has nothing to do with the physical exertion. I disguise it well as I open the door and let Fern go inside first. We're both immediately hit by an aroma that is familiar to anybody who has ever entered a pub that has been in existence for at least fifty years, namely the combined scent of beer, old furniture and the cigarette smoke that has seeped into the walls and long outlived the official indoor smoking ban that came into place in Britain back in 2007. But while Fern might be turning her nose up at it slightly, I like it. To me, this is far better than one of those modern, trendy bars that sprung up all over Manchester the last few years we lived there, and tended to be filled with young yuppies cuddling cocktails.

This is old school.

This is how it used to be.

But as perfect as it is, it is still missing something.

It's missing Alice. She isn't in here either. Then again, there aren't many people in here at all. Just a few elderly men at a table in the corner and some guy at the bar who I can't tell the age of yet because he has his back to us. But he turns around when he hears the squeaking door of the pub closing behind us and, when he does, I see his face, a sight that causes my heart rate to quicken slightly and my hands to get a little sweaty.

It's Rory, Alice's husband.

Thankfully, he has no idea who I am and, of course, I can't let him know that I know who he is. I know his face because I was unable to resist scouring social media for a photo of him back when my affair with Alice began. It might have been a slightly morbid curiosity that had me seeking him out, a way of me discovering what the man who was married to my new lover looked like. Or maybe I was just envious and held some fear that he might be better looking than me. I was quite pleased when that didn't turn out to be the case, and I felt I had him beat in the looks department, in my humble opinion at least. That online 'stalking' I did wasn't purely for reasons of vanity though. It helped me to become comfortable with Rory, at least online anyway, so now when I see him in person, as I knew I would, I can remain calm and not be surprised by anything.

He gives us both a respectable nod and turns back to his beer, and I guess he assumes we're just a couple of tourists stopping for refreshments before we carry on our journey up to Scotland. But we're far more than that, and as we reach the bar and I ask Fern what she wants to drink, I can see him out of the corner of my eye looking again in our direction.

He waits until we have ordered our drinks with the barman before he speaks, and, when he does, I know it will be the start of a rather tricky conversation for me.

'Is that a Manchester accent I detect?'

I confirm that it is, and Rory raises his glass to the two of us.

'Nice to meet you. I'm from there myself, although I call this village home now. Are you guys starting your holiday or heading back home?'

'Actually, we've just moved here,' Fern enlightens him, and Rory looks surprised but thrilled to hear that.

'Really? That's great! Here, have a seat, I'm Rory!'

He gestures to the bar stools next to him before holding out his hand, and though it's extremely uncomfortable for me to have to shake hands with him, I grimace and get through it anyway.

We complete the introductions, but I'm already eyeing up the empty table across the pub because it will be far less awkward for me to enjoy my drink over there rather than here. Fern has already taken a seat at the bar, and now she is asking Rory more about his former life in Manchester. The area he lived in. Where he worked. Does he know that same restaurant we used to eat in? Yes, he does, and the conversation goes on and on as Rory excitedly delivers a brief version of his life story, and we discover we all have plenty in common, the biggest thing now being this new place we call home.

'I was actually born here,' Rory tells us. I already knew that because Alice told me that was why he suggested they make the move here, back when their marriage was encountering difficulties in Manchester. Of course, as far as Rory knows, those difficulties didn't go beyond the both of them not making enough time for each other in the busy city, and if he knew his wife had actually been falling into bed with another man then he might have reacted differently. But, much like Fern, he is operating under the blissful belief that life is good and things work out for the best.

'Do you have a partner?' Fern asks, and I immediately bristle because I'm not sure how I'm going to feel hearing another man talk about being with the woman who I wish was mine.

'The man came out for a quiet beer. Don't be so nosey,' I tell Fern with a chuckle, but Rory has no qualms revealing more to us both.

'Yes, I'm married. My wife's name is Alice. We've been together for over ten years now. You'll have to meet her. I'm sure you'd both get along.'

'That would be lovely,' Fern squeals, barely able to hide her delight, and I'm sure it's because she's thrilled to potentially have a friend her own age here.

'Is Alice at home now?' I ask, trying to make it sound like a casual question rather than one that I'm desperate to know the answer to.

'Yes, she is.'

'And whereabouts is that?'

'Now who's being nosey?' Fern teases me.

'We live on William Street. The little cottage at the end. What about you guys? Where have you moved to? Don't tell me it's that big fancy house overlooking the beach? I know that place has been on the market for a while.'

'That's the one,' I confirm cheerily, pleased to have acquired both Alice's address and also be able to admit to splashing out on what I believe is the best property in the village.

'Wow, that must have cost you a small fortune.'

'It wasn't cheap,' I admit. 'But it was worth every penny.'

Worth every penny to be nearer to Alice again.

'Well, I'm very jealous.'

Oh, you have no idea.

'Well, I'd love to sit here and drink with you all night, but I better be getting back. Alice is making a casserole, and she gets annoyed at me if I'm late.'

Rory finishes his beer then and gets up from his seat but, before he leaves, he makes sure to indicate his interest in making this chat a more regular thing.

'It was great to meet you both. I'm sure you've got lots of things to do at your new home but, once you've settled in, perhaps the four of us could get together for a bite to eat and something to drink. I think it would be fun.'

'That would be wonderful,' Fern exclaims. 'We'd love to.'

'Yeah,' I mutter back between gritted teeth. 'That sounds good.'

I also knew I'd see Rory and be forced to interact with him to some degree when I came here, but that anticipation doesn't mean it's any easier, nor can I say I enjoy a single second of it when it occurs. It was far simpler to hold a conversation with him in my mind than it was in person, that's for sure. But it was just one of the many risks I knew I'd have to run when I made the decision to come here, the same as knowing that, inevitably, Fern and Alice will meet each other at some point. As long as their conversations are kept as short and as civil as the one I've just had with Rory, then everything will be fine.

Rory bids us farewell then and exits the pub, leaving me and Fern at the bar, nursing what's left of our drinks.

'You've barely touched yours,' she observes, nodding at my full glass. 'Is everything okay?'

'Everything's fine,' I reply before forcing myself to take a sip, and I mean it. Now that Rory has gone, I no longer have to pretend to be friendly with a guy I am envious of.

He doesn't know how lucky he is to be married to a woman like Alice. It shows because, if he was, why on earth was he sitting here in the pub when he could have been at home with her?

I'm not going to feel bad about what I'm going to take from

him, not if he doesn't appreciate it. I'm just going to carry on with my plan.

I'm going to get Alice back.

FIVE

FERN

It's Drew's first day at the practice today, so I'm in the new house with nothing but the remaining unpacked boxes to keep me company. I manage to make it through the morning without too much trouble because there is a lot to sort out upstairs, including trying to rebuild the spare bed we have that was dismantled back in Manchester. The main bed has already been put together, a task we did after getting back from the pub and one that was made harder because fiddling around with nuts and bolts is not easy after a couple of drinks. By the time the bed was made, the two of us had collapsed onto it, exhausted from the day's endeavours, though sleep only came easily for one of us.

Drew's snoring told me he was at rest, but I lay awake for hours until sleep eventually came for me and, when it did, I didn't hear Drew leave the house this morning, although that's not unusual.

He's always been quiet leaving for work, and I'm not a morning person.

I know why I struggled to sleep. *It was this place.* I've tried to ignore it since I woke up, but the silence and the solitude of the empty house starts to get a little too much for me by the afternoon. Despite playing some music on my phone to break it up a bit, I can't help but feel it's still there, lingering in the background, gnawing away at me like a problem that can't be ignored.

I'm used to hearing lorries rumbling past, sirens blaring, and car horns tooting. I'm accustomed to the sound of aeroplanes overhead and trains in the distance, screeching over the tracks on their way into a crowded station full of people. I'd normally hear the voices of some of those people, some chatting on their phones, others laughing loudly between themselves or shouting out to get another person's attention. Children skipping home from school, adults trudging to and from work, delivery drivers reversing in the street because they've got lost and can't find the right address.

Noise. Commotion. *Action.*

No amount of music can distract me from the fact that if I was to turn the song off now, I would hear nothing. Not a single sound. Not even a damn seagull, and even that annoys me because they should be around here somewhere, considering the close proximity to the water.

You know you're going mad when you start getting annoyed at birds.

I first realised the silence was a problem as we were lying in bed last night after getting home from the pub. Drew had no problems falling asleep beside me, no doubt helped by the beer he had consumed as well as the lethargy from the pizza we ordered not long after we got back from the village pub. But I had great difficulty in resting, and the longer I lay there listening to absolutely nothing at all, the worse I started to feel about things.

Regret is a strong word, and one many people like to shy away from, but I have no problems facing the subject. That's why I spent several hours during the night pondering whether or not I had done the right thing in moving here with Drew. By dawn, I'd dropped off and missed seeing Drew get dressed for work, putting on one of those smart suits of his as he prepared to go and do what he does best. If I had been awake then I would have made sure to pretend like everything was fine. I would have kissed him goodbye and told him I'd see him later, and he would have left without any clue that I had actually been awake most of the night wondering what I have gotten myself into. I'm still unsure if I regret coming here or not, but I'm positive the answer will reveal itself to me in the coming days and weeks. Until then, I'm stuck with the choice between being here in this house, ticking off one tedious task after the other, or getting outside and enjoying some fresh air.

In the end, there's no contest.

Fastening up the laces on my hiking boots and pulling up the zipper on my raincoat, I am determined to give this new location of mine a good go, and what better way to do that than to head out for a walk on the beach? The sky is grey, and the wind is strong enough to add a chill to the air, but I'm not going to be put off by that and, once I'm outside, I set off in the direction of the water.

Easily crossing the quiet road at the front of the house, I have soon swapped the concrete for sand, and that was not something I could say I ever did back in Manchester. While living there, the only time I ever set foot on a beach was during the two or three weeks a year we would jet off to somewhere warm like Greece or Italy, or occasionally somewhere further afield, like Barbados. Drew and I have had many great holidays over the years, but we haven't been abroad at all in the past year. And holiday plans were indefinitely put on hold when he suddenly started talking about making a dramatic house move. I'm on a beach now and, while walking in boots is not quite the same as having the sand beneath my toes, it's better than nothing.

I grimace as the icy January wind whips around me while I march on down to the water's edge, not failing to notice that I'm the only person for a long way in either direction. There's not even a solitary dogwalker in sight, which only adds to my feeling of loneliness the further I go.

I journey on, determined to keep going until I discover exactly why so many people covet this kind of lifestyle away from all other human beings, but by the time I make it to where the water meets the sand, I still have no idea why people like this. I've never felt more isolated in my entire life, and the yawning chasm of this part of the coastline seems to be mocking me, as I stand on the edge of it and stare out into the abyss.

I think about all the things that had to happen to lead to me being here and, of course, the main thing that had to happen was me meeting Drew in the first place. Our paths crossed at a Christmas party in a large marquee in Manchester, one of those types of work events where several companies had all paid to hold their annual festivities in the same place. That meant there were all sorts of employees together, from salespeople, admin officers, accountants, hospitality staff and, as I would soon discover, *doctors*. It was quite the thrill for me and my colleagues at the time to discover that the table full of handsome men were all in the medical profession and, once the boring meal was out of the way, everybody hit the dance floor, providing me with a better opportunity to mingle. I had my eyes on several dishy men and was excited for any fun that night, being single and in my twenties, when I was offered a glass of champagne by a man dancing beside me. I accepted, not just because I was thirsty but because the person offering it looked incredibly hot in a tuxedo. As we chatted, I learnt his name was Drew, he was a doctor and, most importantly of all, he was single.

The best I was hoping for at that point was a kiss, or maybe a little more, but I was certainly not expecting us to end up in a serious relationship. I didn't think a man with such a prestigious career as his would ever be interested in a woman like me, with a bland and basic job, beyond a quick snog and a fumble in the back of a taxi. But that was where Drew surprised me, because he was super-engaged with me, interested in everything I had to say and, learning more about me, proving it further when he asked me for my phone number so he could make sure he had a way of seeing me again. And that was how I became a doctor's wife, well, once he'd proposed and got me down the aisle, of course, but that was a mere formality after we had spent several months growing closer and I realised I hadn't just snared myself a handsome man, but an honest, hardworking and humble one too.

To think that my life would be very different if I hadn't gone to that Christmas party or accepted that glass of champagne. But I did and here I am. While that night started things for me and Drew, it's not the main reason I am here, and as I stare out across the water, I consider the other factors that contributed to me ending up in a place like Arberness, and there is one overriding one that trumps all else.

The real reason I came here is a secret, one that nobody is aware of, especially not my husband.

Drew has his secrets, and I have mine, and my secret is this:

I know all about his affair with Alice.

I found out about it in Manchester, and that's how I knew exactly why he wanted to move to this village. He's moved to be nearer to *her*, presumably so he can restart the relationship again. Like the fool that he is, he thinks I'm still in the dark about all of it, but I've known for a long time.

So why haven't I told him what I know?

Perhaps more importantly, why am I still with him?

I might be stupid, but I'm trying to give my husband a

chance. Of course, I was heartbroken when I discovered he had another woman, but after finding out that she had moved away, I had hoped he would see the error of his ways and choose to be faithful to me again. Then he suggested we move house, and of all the places he could have picked, he chose to come here, where she was, showing to me that he hadn't changed or seen the error of his ways at all.

I'm still giving him a chance, though. Just because he is in the same place as Alice again, it doesn't mean they are going to be getting up to their old tricks. They still have a choice. They don't have to cheat on me or Rory, Alice's poor partner, who I pretended I didn't know when I met him the other day. That pair of liars still have a chance to save themselves. Whether they do the right thing or not remains to be seen.

But for their sakes, I really hope they do.

I step forward so that the edges of my boots are in the water and, once they are, I stand and let the current wash away the grains of sand that are stuck to the sides of them. Pretty soon, my boots are clean, but my mind can't be cleansed quite so easily. All I can picture is him and her together, laughing behind my back, thinking they are getting away with it.

Perhaps I should have stayed in Manchester. Maybe I should never have come here? I could have just demanded a divorce and left the pair of them to it.

But I chose this option. I chose to come here. I chose to keep playing the game.

And because of that, there's no telling what might happen next.

SIX

DREW

So far, so good. Being a doctor in a place like this is infinitely easier than being a doctor in the city. For a start, there is no overcrowded waiting room on the other side of my closed surgery door, lowering my mood every time the door opens and I steal a quick glimpse outside. Instead, all I have seen during the course of today has been several plastic chairs, nearly all of which have remained unoccupied, proving that not only are there not many people in this village, but there aren't many sick ones either. A knock-on effect of that is less paperwork for me to do, because there can be no prescriptions to sign or referral letters to type if there's hardly anybody coming through the door, can there?

My hands have never had it so easy and have spent most of the time sitting in my lap rather than typing on a keyboard or reaching for a pen. Come to think of it, my stethoscope has enjoyed an easy ride too, because it's been lying on my desk all day and hasn't been picked up once, which is certainly a rarity.

The biggest problem in my last workplace was that there were too many patients and too few doctors. But while it would be nice to have a colleague or two here who I could chat about the medical profession with over a coffee, the fact I am the only doctor in the village proves how undemanding this place is. I almost chuckled to myself earlier when I imagined my former colleagues back in the city still swamped with all the check-ups they were having to perform, while I sat here with my feet up on my desk, an apple between my teeth and the pages of a newspaper open in front of me.

I'm surprised the doctor that I replaced here even bothered to retire. He might as well have kept on collecting a steady paycheque because this is hardly demanding work, and while he's probably on a golf course somewhere right now, I bet I'm just as chilled as he is.

I have done some work today to stave off the danger of my medical qualifications starting to go to waste. My first patient was a young mother who wanted me to take a look at her five-year-old son, because she was worried his tongue looked a strange colour, and she'd read rather a lot online about meningitis and wondered if that particular illness was manifesting itself in her child's mouth. I was happy to inform her that she had absolutely nothing to worry about, and that her son's tongue looked perfectly normal, before wondering aloud if perhaps a trip to the dentist might be a better plan. It was obvious her child had been enjoying rather a lot of sweets in his short time on this earth.

A few more patients had trickled in after that, including an elderly woman who seemed like she had come to see me just to have somebody to talk to, and an overweight man who complained that his back was hurting him, only to then admit that it might have something to do with having spent all of last weekend digging out the flowerbed in his garden. I gave the woman what she needed, which was a ten-minute chat and a couple of smiles to remind her that she wasn't so alone after all, while I got rid of the man by telling him to take it easy for a few

days and leave the gardening to somebody a little more accustomed to physical exercise.

I'm aware that with more days like this one I run the risk of
getting bored at some point, but I didn't move here to be
mentally stimulated, or at least not workwise anyway.

I'm seeking out my stimulation in far more exciting ways.

Lunchtime came and went, and for the first time in ages, I
actually got to enjoy a full break and even made it away from
my desk and out into the fresh air for a short walk. Not at all like
in the city where I would scoff a sandwich and a packet of crisps
in between appointments, and awkwardly brush crumbs off my
shirt while asking about my patients' bowel movement habits.

After my break, I spent several minutes making chit-chat with
the receptionist here, Julie, a woman who looked very bored at
being stationed in such a quiet surgery, only for me to make her feel
more grateful about her lot in life after I filled her head with horror
stories from my time spent working in Manchester. She only had to
hear my tales of what it was like to work in a doctor's surgery there
to realise that she wouldn't have lasted five minutes in that kind of
environment. The afternoon ticked along at a reasonable pace, and
now the clock tells me the end of the working day is nigh. With an
empty waiting room out there and no more patients to see, I guess
that means I've made it through my first day here unscathed.

And then I get a phone call.

'Hi, Drew. We've just had a last-minute walk in, and I was
wondering if you could see them. They don't have an appointment though, so let me know if it's too much trouble, and I can
ask them to come back tomorrow.'

Julie's nervous tone makes me smile because, while she
might be worrying that I'm going to be too busy if I take one
more patient today, the truth is I've never enjoyed such an easy
day in my whole career. That's why I tell her not to be silly and
to send the unexpected patient in straight away, because I'll

happily take a look at them before logging off my computer and hanging my dusty stethoscope up until tomorrow. Before I can close my newspaper and at least pretend like I've been relatively busy in here, the door to my surgery swings open without so much as a warning knock, and when I look up to see who has entered, it's as if all the air is suddenly sucked from the room.

It's her.

The woman I moved here for.

Alice.

'Oh my God, it's true,' Alice says as she sees me sitting at my desk.

I'm quickly out of my seat and rushing towards her, firstly to close the door so that Julie can't hear us talk, but secondly because I want to be as close to her as possible now that I have found her again. But she found me first, and she doesn't look happy, not that a frown on her face can detract too much from her appearance, at least in my eyes anyway.

High cheekbones, a cute button nose and eyes so green they make me think of the countryside, and all of it framed by a head of luscious blonde locks, the colour and the volume of it the thing that drew my attention to her in the first place. I told Alice that she could be a model once while we were lying in bed together and she laughed at me, but I wasn't joking. She really is that beautiful, and her choosing to be with me made me feel like I was some kind of ancient explorer who had unearthed a hidden treasure that the rest of the world was yet to discover the true beauty of.

'What the hell are you doing here?' she asks me just before I manage to close the door. I pray that Julie didn't hear that question.

'Alice, hi, how have you been?'

'What are you doing here?'

Not quite the welcome I was hoping for, but I should try and see this from her point of view. It must be a little overwhelming.

'I understand this is a bit of a surprise, but just take a seat, and I'll explain everything,' I say, looking to reassure her, and I attempt to touch her arm then, but she moves away from me. She didn't completely recoil at my touch, which would have been awful, but she did flinch slightly, which is still bad. That's because this is the woman who used to melt in my arms as we lay in bed together, and the thought that she may never feel the same way about me again makes my heart ache. But it's still very early days here. She's still trying to process all of this, so I'll give her as much space as she needs.

'Why are you here?'

Alice's question is spoken in a more hushed tone than the last one, which I am grateful for and take as evidence that she is calming down slightly, or at least keeping the presence of mind that giving the receptionist something to gossip about is not a good idea in a place as small as this one.

'You know why I'm here,' I say calmly and with the hint of a smile. 'I'm here for us.'

'There is no us! Not anymore!'

'There can be. We can start again. Pick up where we left off. Just say the word.'

I might be coming across as needy, but this is the time to lay all my cards out on the table. No point dancing around the point. I just need to state what I want and why I want it.

But Alice isn't taking it well.

'I can't believe you did this. I can't believe you followed me!'

Alice starts pacing around the room while I remain standing by the door, and part of me is maintaining that position because I'm afraid she is going to run out of here before we've had the chance to talk things through.

It wouldn't be difficult for me to stop her if she did try to leave before I was ready for her to, considering she's barely five foot four and is extremely slender. I could pick her up and carry her if I so wished, not that I've ever tried.

'Rory came home from the pub last night and told me he'd met a couple from Manchester who had just moved to the area,' Alice says, still moving around with urgency. 'When he told me the names, I could hardly believe it. Then when he said you were a doctor, I just knew it was you. But I had to come down here to see it with my own eyes. So, it's true. You really have moved here. You're insane!'

'No, I'm not insane. I'm in love. In love with you, Alice, and I know you feel the same way about me because you've said those same exact words to me before, remember?'

'That was a long time ago! Things have changed now!'

'How have they changed?'

'I told you I wanted to do the right thing by Rory. Stop lying to him. Make another go of it. When he suggested we move here, I knew it was what we needed. And it's worked. Things are fine between us now.'

'Fine? Is that all you want from a relationship? Just fine?'

'We're not kids, Drew, we're adults! We can't play games and act on our whims. We have to grow up, and that's what I did by moving here. Now you've followed me and ruined everything!'

This is not going at all how I had dreamed about our reunion going in my head. In my fantasies, Alice took me turning up here as a huge declaration of love and kissed me passionately. But I guess this isn't like the movies. This is quickly turning into a nightmare, and if I'm not careful, the only thing I'm going to be left with is a broken heart, a very boring job in a village and the knowledge that the woman I really love can't stand the sight of me.

'Alice, please, just sit down for a moment and let me explain why I did this,' I try again and, thankfully, this time she does what I ask.

Alice takes a seat in the plastic chair by my desk that is usually reserved for patients, while I sit down in my comfier office chair and take a deep breath before taking another shot at it.

'I know why you ended things between us, and I know why you moved away,' I begin, talking slowly and quietly, as if delivering bad test results to a concerned patient. 'And I tried to let you go and move on, I really did. But I couldn't stop thinking about you. About us. About how good we were together. All the fun times we had and all the plans we used to make when we'd talk about the things we could do if we weren't encumbered by our partners. No matter how hard I tried, I just couldn't forget. It began eating away at me, the thought of Rory up here with you. The thought of you settling for him instead of me. And the thought that I could go the rest of my life wondering what if, until I was an old man lying on my sick bed, full of regrets and thinking about what might have been.'

Alice goes to speak, but I hold up my hand to let her know that I'm not finished, and she has to hear all of it before she can make an informed decision.

'So I came up with a plan. I thought about moving here, and while it was just a pipe dream in the early stages, once I read that the village was going to be needing a new doctor, it felt like the universe was telling me something. I applied for the job, and when I got it, I knew I couldn't go back. I persuaded Fern that we should move, and here we are. I know it's a shock, but understand that I came here with the intention of rekindling what we had. You know I'll do whatever it takes to make you happy. You know that, right? Because I love you, Alice. And I've come to realise that I always will.'

With my well-rehearsed speech over with, I brace myself for the response. But it takes a moment to come because Alice is just looking at me with what can only be described as disbelief in her eyes.

'I'm sorry,' she says eventually, breaking the silence, but also making it seem like she is going to go on to break my heart. 'You shouldn't have come here. You're wasting your time, and you're risking both of our marriages in the process. Whatever you came here to do, I need you to forget about it because it's not going to happen.'

Alice gets up, and while I try to slow her down and change her mind, it doesn't work.

'Please, if you love me as much as you say you do then you'll respect my wishes,' she says, looking every bit as sad as I feel inside. Then she walks away, out of my surgery and seemingly out of my life just like she did once before.

And all I can think is that I have made a very big mistake.

SEVEN

FERN

With the working day over and Drew due home any minute, I'm getting to work on reheating the lasagne that Audrey kindly gave to us yesterday. I'm so glad I don't have to cook anything yet because the beautiful kitchen is still very much in a state of disrepair, with half-unpacked boxes of utensils everywhere, so this generous gift from our new neighbour is helping me out big time. It's still not as easy as it should be to get some hot food onto a plate. The messy house and my anxious state of mind, over what my husband might be up to now that he is back in the same place as Alice, means that I'm making silly mistakes.

For example, it took me a lot longer than it should have to figure out that the reason the microwave wasn't doing a very good job of heating up the food inside it was because I hadn't bothered to put the plug into the wall and turn the power on. Much like how I decided to try and make some homemade garlic bread to accompany the lasagne, only to realise that I had neither garlic nor any ingredients that could be used to make bread. I'll need to sharpen up a little bit before Drew walks through the front door, because I can't have him noticing I'm distracted and for him to start asking questions of me. I need him to keep thinking that I am still the loyal, dutiful and, most of all, oblivious wife for as long as possible, or at least until I know what his plans are with Alice.

By the time I hear the key in the door, the lasagne is piping hot, and I've dug out a bottle of red wine from one of the boxes to open, allowing two glasses to be poured that will help take the edge off things, for both of us I suspect.

'How was your first day, darling?' I ask my husband as he enters the kitchen and throws his suit jacket over one of the boxes.

'It was okay,' he responds in a weary tone, suggesting it was anything but.

'What happened? Don't tell me it was busy? There can't be more sick people here than in Manchester, can there?'

'No, there isn't. It was quiet.'

'Oh, I see. Too quiet?'

'I wouldn't say that. It'll just take some getting used to, that's all.'

'Well, you can tell me all about it while we eat. Here, this one's yours.'

I hand a plate with a very generous wedge of lasagne on it to Drew, before gesturing to one of the glasses of wine on the side as well.

'I thought we could have a little drink with our dinner. Toast to you and your new job.'

'Great,' Drew replies with all the enthusiasm of someone who has just been told that this will be the last meal they ever get to savour, so they better make the most of it.

I keep my eye on him as he slumps down into one of the chairs at our mahogany dining table, which we brought from our old house, before he begins prodding at his meal with a fork, and it's obvious that something is very wrong in his world, although I'm still not sure what it is. Is it to do with work, or has something already happened with Alice? He'll never tell me the truth if it is the latter, I suppose, but that doesn't mean I can't pry a little and, at worst, make him feel as uncomfortable as he deserves to feel after what he's done to me.

'Tell me all about it then,' I say as I take my seat opposite him and slide one of the glasses of wine in his direction. 'How many patients did you see?'

'Seven.'

'Oh, that's not too bad, is it? A nice gentle start.'

I make my own start on my food then, popping the first piece of lasagne in my mouth and, as I'd expected, it's delicious.

'I suppose.'

'And was everybody nice?'

'Yeah, I guess.'

'Did anybody welcome you to the village?'

'A few of them did.'

'That's good. Everyone is so friendly here, aren't they?'

'Yeah.'

If I had to describe Drew's demeanour, I'd say he's acting very much like a moody teenager who has just been told to stop playing his video games upstairs and come down to join the rest of the family at the dining table. The fact that Drew is a man of forty, wearing a shirt and tie, having completed a day doing a very serious job, and is now sitting in the rather expensive home that he has to pay the mortgage on, means he is far from a moody teenager. He's a grown-up with responsibilities, which means this whole disposition of his is rather disconcerting.

'Was anybody rude to you today?' I ask, wondering if that might be the cause of his bad mood. 'I know you had some horrible patients in Manchester. Are there a couple of bad ones up here too?'

'No, everyone's been all right with me,' Drew replies, but he's now started stabbing at his food a little more aggressively, suggesting that he's feeling worse about things, not better.

'How's your receptionist? What's her name?'

'Julie.'

'Is she nice?'

'Yeah, fine.'

I think I would actually get more words out of a moody teenager if this conversation carries on in a similar vein.

'Okay, so work was fine, which means something else must be bothering you. So, what is it?'

I put my knife and fork down then and wait for the answer, showing Drew that he has my undivided attention. That gesture forces him to stop eating, and when he looks up at me, he looks a little awkward.

'It's nothing, don't worry about it.'

'No, come on. I want to know. Something is clearly on your mind so tell me what it is. Is it the food? The wine? Something else I've done?'

'No.'

'Then what?'

Drew lets out a deep sigh before putting his own utensils down and taking a large glug of wine, as if he needs the extra courage from the alcohol before he finally gets around to enlightening me.

'Do you think we did the right thing moving here?'

'Excuse me?'

'Us. This village. This house. Leaving Manchester. Do you think we did the right thing?'

'It's a bit late to ask that now.'

My abrupt tone causes Drew to flinch slightly.

'I know. I'm sorry. Never mind.'

Drew tries to go back to eating then, but I don't let him.

'If there's a problem then you need to tell me.'

'There's no problem.'

'Are you sure? Because it seems like there is.'

'I'm just tired. I guess it's the stress of everything. All the goodbyes and the hellos. All the upheaval of the move. My new job. Wanting to fit in and make a good impression. I guess I just wasn't prepared for how draining it would all be.'

I study my husband's face to try and see if he is telling me the truth, but, as always, he is difficult to read. But not quite as difficult to read as he thinks he is.

'You think we might have made a mistake?'

'I didn't say that.'

'But you're thinking it?'

'No, I'm not.'

Drew laughs then, presumably to try and break the tension that had been building in the room ever since he walked in, before he asks me how my day was. I fill him in about the progress of the unpacking before mentioning my walk on the beach.

'That sounds nice,' he tells me through a mouthful of meat and sauce.

'Yeah, it was,' I lie, but he sees right through that one because, unlike him, I have to really make the effort when I speak an untruth, and I obviously wasn't trying as hard as I should have been.

'What's wrong? You're not enjoying it here?'

'I didn't say that.'

'I can sense there's something.'

'It's just very quiet, especially when I'm here on my own all day. I guess I never felt lonely in the city, knowing there were so many people in any given direction.'

'Audrey's next door. You've got her.'

'That's not quite the same.'

'I'm sorry, I was joking. How about you go into the village tomorrow? It'll get you out of the house for a bit, and you're bound to get chatting to a few locals there.'

'Yeah, I might do.'

We carry on eating in silence until we're both finished. Drew offers to do the washing up, and I don't protest. While he's busy at the sink, lamenting the fact that we haven't sorted out the dishwasher in this new place yet, I look at his jacket on the top of the box and wonder if his phone is in there. More specifically, I'm wondering if he might have been messaging Alice, but I can't know for sure without taking a look for myself.

I decide not to risk it while he's in the same room as me, and hope I might get the opportunity to take a peek at his device after he's gone upstairs to have a shower. He does leave the room after completing the washing up, and I'm just about to go and do some investigating when he returns and says he forgot to take his jacket, killing my chances of getting a moment alone with his phone.

'It's not like you to tidy up after yourself,' I muse as he scoops up his jacket and, with it, his mobile, but he just sighs and tells me the house is already untidy enough without him adding to the mess. Then he leaves the kitchen, and as I listen to him trudging up the stairs, I wonder if he came back for his phone because there is something on there he doesn't want to risk me seeing.

And so it starts all over again. The life of a wife who can't trust her husband. I wouldn't wish this on anyone. But if the affair is going to start again, then one thing is for certain.

I wouldn't wish what is going to happen to Drew on anyone either.

EIGHT

DREW

There's a lot of irritations when attempting to settle into a new home, and one of them is trying to get the correct water temperature in the shower. Despite thinking I had figured it out yesterday, it seems I can't quite get it right this time and, despite a lot of twiddling and fiddling, the water is either way too hot or way too cold.

On any other day, this would be mildly annoying.

After today, it's downright infuriating.

'Come on, damn it!' I cry as I hit the tiled wall with the palm of my hand before trying again, until I'm suddenly scalded by the water after almost being frozen by it a second ago. 'You stupid thing!' I shout as my temper boils over, and it's no surprise when I hear a knock on the bathroom door, followed by Fern's voice as she asks me if everything is okay.

'I'm fine!' I shout over the roar of the water as it rings around my ears and splashes by my feet. Finally, after much effort, I find the perfect temperature. It's just a shame I had to slightly injure my hand and have my wife come and check on me in the process.

It's a minor victory, but I'll take it, and as I start to wash myself, I try to remember that what I have suffered today is only a setback and not the final result. Okay, so Alice didn't respond well to finding out I had moved to the village, but I'll put that down to how unexpected it must have been for her to see me and give her some leeway. She just needs a few days to get her head around it, and once the dust has settled, she'll realise what a show of affection I have made. I expect, or at least hope, that will be the moment when she reconsiders and returns to talk to me again.

Until then, I'm stranded in a sort of no man's land, unable to go forward or back, completely at the mercy of another person's decision. If Alice calms down and decides that she is interested in giving us another go then everything will be okay. But if she doesn't, which is my biggest fear in life right now, I have absolutely no idea what my next move will be. All I know is that I'll be stuck in a tiny village so close to yet so far from the woman I want to be with, and potentially condemned to a lifetime of misery, eking out my days treating the residents of this village and coming home to a woman who is pleasant enough but no longer sets my world on fire.

As I have often found myself doing in the past, I wish that Fern could make me feel like Alice does. Things would be so much easier then. There would have never been a need for telling lies, sneaking around and keeping my phone close by so she couldn't snoop at it. And there certainly wouldn't have been a need to move here, to this place, to this house, to this unfamiliar shower.

The things we do for true love, hey?

Alas, my wife has never been able to ignite in me the fire that burns whenever I'm around Alice. I thought she was everything I needed in a woman, I really did, but then I met Alice and realised Fern hadn't even come close. The strength of feeling I experience when with the two differs greatly and there was no comparison.

Alice does it for me.
In hindsight, Fern never did.

I don't plan on getting out of this shower anytime soon because once I do leave the bathroom, I'll have to go back to pretending to Fern that I'm fine. Watch some TV with her. Make small talk during the ad breaks. Sip on a boring cup of tea while trying not to stare at my phone in case Alice decides that she wants to get in touch.

Maybe that's it. I should call her or at least send her a message. Reach out instead of leaving things as they are. But doing that would run the risk of her not responding to me, and I don't want that because it'll only make me seem weak and desperate. She has all the power in this situation, but I don't want to make that glaringly obvious. Better to stay quiet and let her mind begin to wonder as she thinks about what I might be up to. Sure, I might be sitting by the phone like a loser hoping she texts me, but she doesn't have to know that. She might imagine me having fun with Fern, maybe making love, and hopefully that will make Alice jealous and stir up some of those old feelings that she has obviously done a very good job of stuffing way down inside.

I know Alice used to get curious about whether I was still being intimate with my wife while I was seeing her and, while I was barely getting physical with Fern during that time, I occasionally hinted that I had been just because I knew it drove Alice wild and made her want me even more. Looking back on it now, it seems childish to have played games like that, but I did it, and I enjoyed it at the time, probably because it always got me more of what I wanted, which was *her*.

It's scary to admit to myself, but I've never wanted anything as much as Alice. Not money, not power, not respect. I don't give a damn about nice cars or big houses anymore, although I'm well aware this house is hardly tiny, and I'm not exactly driving to work in a dilapidated vehicle. Nor do I care about other things that people might generally strive for, and that includes starting a family. I'd rather be childless with Alice than have kids with Fern or any other woman. I'm just glad my wife has not brought up that subject for a while now.

At forty, time is not on Fern's side when it comes to that, and while I do feel a little guilty about spending what is presumably the last part of her biological window obsessing over another woman, I am actually relieved we didn't have any kids of our own earlier. That would have only complicated things. I have had a hard enough time as it is keeping my other life secret from one person. No need to add one or two young-sters into the mix and complicate this marriage even further. It was easy to manage during the first nine years of our matri-mony, but I wasn't leading a double life then. The second another woman came on the scene was the moment I realised all those vows I had said in front of over a hundred of our loved ones and in the eyes of God meant very little in practice.

However, I have wondered why Fern stopped talking about the prospect of parenthood over these last few six months or so, but, if I had to guess, I think it's because she realises it might not happen now, so she is protecting herself from too much hurt by still talking about it. That's a shame, as there was a time when that was what we both wanted. But that was a time when I had no idea what it was I truly wanted in life and thought the stan-dard partner, two kids and decent career could cut it. Little did I realise I was missing out on so much passion and fun, though at least I figured that out in the end. But Fern no longer bringing up the subject of children helps me out because it means I don't have to come up with excuses about why I don't want to be physical with her at key times of the month, nor do I have to cause her even more distress one day in the future if I finally get to be with Alice. But that is a big if, because even if Alice changes her mind and says she wants me again, I know I can't leave Fern. It's not as simple as that. There's a reason I'm still with her and it's not just because I feel duty-bound as a husband.

But it's a reason I don't like to think about too much.

I wish I could stay in this shower all night, but Fern will get suspicious soon and start banging on the door again, so I reluctantly turn the water off but not before I have made a mental note of exactly which position I had the dials in, so there's no drama with tomorrow night's shower. Then, after drying off and throwing on a T-shirt and an old pair of sweatpants, I join my wife downstairs on the sofa, where I find her flicking through the channels with the remote control and asking me what I fancy watching.

'I'm easy,' I tell her as I sneak a peek at my phone and feel the disappointment deep inside when I see that Alice has not bothered to get in touch with me yet.

'I can't decide. I need your opinion.'

'I'm not bothered. I'll watch anything.'

'It would be nice if you helped.'

'It doesn't matter. Just pick a channel and stick with it!'

'Why are you yelling at me?'

'I'm not yelling!'

Fern shakes her head at me before storming out of the room, and while I regret what's just happened, I don't have the energy to go after her and apologise. I'd much rather get out of this house and get some fresh air, so that's exactly what I do. Despite shouting upstairs to ask Fern if she wants to come with me, she doesn't respond.

'Fine, suit yourself,' I mutter under my breath, before I leave the house and start pacing down the street in the direction of the village centre.

I'm not walking with any particular destination in mind; I'm just walking because it increases the chances of what I might see or, rather, *who I might see*. Would it be a bad thing if I was to bump into Alice and get another go at talking to her? I don't think so. And even if I don't get to speak with her, just a glimpse of her would be nice and brighten up what has quickly turned into a terrible evening.

Despite walking all around the village for the better part of an hour, I don't see Alice anywhere, my efforts not aided by the early setting of the sun at this time of year, and I know it's a lost cause. Wandering listlessly back home, I make a stop off on the beach to throw a few pebbles into the water and try and find some solace in the stars above. But it still doesn't cheer me up much. That's why I turn my attentions to my phone, typing out a private message to Alice on one of her social media accounts, in which I say I'm sorry for surprising her earlier but that I'm not sorry for what I have done because love is worth risking it all in the end.

I pace around nervously on the beach as I pray for a reply, but it never comes, and as I wander back off the sand and onto the concrete, under a black sky, any optimism I had about this working out okay has faded as quickly as the weak winter sun that once faintly glowed on the horizon.

Fern says nothing to me when I get home, choosing to ignore me as she watches some documentary about chimpanzees in the wild. If only she'd just put that on before then we could have saved ourselves an argument, I think, but I dare not say that to her. Instead, I just slump down on the sofa opposite her and keep checking my phone.

But when the time comes for us to go upstairs to bed, I've got the same treatment from Alice as I have from Fern.

Silence.

NINE

FERN

Last night was no fun. I could tell that Drew was in a bad mood almost as soon as he walked through the door, and nothing that happened after that changed my mind. After an awkward meal, a very long shower and an argument, which resulted in me stomping upstairs while he stormed out of the house, we ended up sleeping in the same bed, although I didn't fail to notice that, despite being close to one another physically, there was a huge distance mentally. Now he's back at work, and I'm by myself again, although not for long. That's because I'm going to take his advice and go into the village today and, as it's a Wednesday, there's a certain coffee morning that I am planning on attending.

The walk into the centre of the village is a quick and pain- less one. No hills to climb, no long waits to cross the road, just a bit of rain to contend with, but it's nothing that my trusty umbrella can't handle. It's a relief to make it to the main street and see a bit of activity around these parts, even if it is only in the form of a large truck delivering a load of beer kegs to the pub and a postman chatting to a dogwalker across the road. It's not much, but it's the most action I've seen in any one area for the past few days. If I close my eyes and listen to the kegs being unloaded rather noisily, I could almost be back in the city.

Almost.

I'm not exactly sure where to find the church hall that is hosting the coffee morning, but I figure I'll find it easily enough in a tiny place like this, if I'm willing to look and, sure enough, I do. It's a small building tucked around the side of the only grocery shop in town. Like every other building in the centre of this village, its architecture suggests it is steeped in history and was built centuries ago, not that the old stonework makes the place unattractive. It adds character, admittedly much more than one finds in a modern city, so it's one plus point to this place, I suppose. But it's not as if more modern amenities haven't been able to reach even this part of the world, because surrounding the antiquated village centre are all the new and hugely expensive houses that have sprung up in recent times, homes that have made this place extremely attractive to wealthy people looking to retire or buy a second property and let it out as a holiday home. And, of course, a few of the internationally known business franchises have set up shop here, certain places that specialise in coffee or fast food, clearly not content with dominating the market in places like Los Angeles, New York and Tokyo and feeling the need to squeeze a little profit out of a place like Arberness too.

I see a poster advertising the coffee morning stuck to the inside of the window as I approach the front door and, after checking my watch, I see that I am a few minutes early. But the door is already open and, not wanting to wait outside in the rain any longer, I decide to go in and see if anybody is there.

As I walk into the room, I count at least six people standing over by the long table that's draped in a white tablecloth, and I can see that all of them are helping with setting out the cups and saucers for this morning's event. One of the group is Audrey, and she gives me a wave when she sees me before telling me how glad she is that I came, and then wastes no time in introducing me to the other women in attendance.

I'm met with a barrage of names and friendly smiles, and I shake several hands and receive a warm welcome to the village. There's a Dorothy and an Ethel, and I think there is a Margaret in there too. As for the other names, I've already forgotten them because my brain simply can't remember that many new names at once. Everybody seems nice, which is the main thing, although I can't help but notice that I seem to be the youngest in the room by at least thirty years. But then I see a flash of blonde hair in my peripheral vision, and as I turn to see who is entering the room, it's clear there is now somebody here who is much closer to my own age.

And it's somebody I recognise.

It's Alice.

Despite knowing that she was going to be here after Audrey told me about her, and despite psyching myself up ahead of the move to this village so I would be more prepared for this moment, it's still hard to contain the mixture of emotions that I feel now that I'm in her presence. This is the woman who has stolen my husband's heart from me, a heart that I cherished with every part of my own at one time; and the true extent of Drew's lies meant that the breaking of my own heart was painful when it occurred.

Despite knowing about what Drew did with this woman back in Manchester, and having all the time since to try and process it, it's still hard not to compare myself to her.

I'd say she's prettier than me, and not just because she clearly makes more of an effort with her hair and make-up than I do. No, she has a natural beauty, one that I've never had and, because of that, she carries herself with a confidence that I've never possessed either. She moves effortlessly, as if life has always come easily to her, and maybe it has. I imagine she is the kind of woman who is used to getting what she wants when she looks as good as that. As she makes her way through the room, grinning and greeting a few of the other attendees, I find myself wanting to slap that smile off her face and tell all these other women exactly who they are being friendly with. But I don't do that because it'll ruin everything, so I just turn back to the table and help set out a few more cups and saucers, pretending to be busy and waiting for Alice to come to me.

But she doesn't do that. She keeps her distance, and I suspect it's because her husband already mentioned the new couple in the village to her, and she knows exactly who I am. How can she not know me? Drew will have told her about me during their affair, and for all I know she's looked at photos of me online and sized up her rival, just like I have done with her. She may have already seen Drew since we arrived, for all I know, so it's no wonder she might be feeling a little awkward now that I'm here.

It's the thought of making her uncomfortable that allows me to switch my mindset and go from being the one who feels like the victim to being the one who might be able to exert a little control in this situation. Alice knows who I am, but she doesn't know that I know who she is, so why not have a little fun with her?

I finish setting up the cups and offer to help Audrey with the box of biscuits that she is tearing into, but she tells me that she is fine, so I move closer to Alice, who is working on setting out several chairs in a small semi-circle.

'Hi, need a hand?'

Alice almost drops the chair she is carrying when she hears my question before composing herself and forcing a smile onto her face.

'Oh, erm, yes, that would be great, thank you.'

She nods towards a stack of chairs, and I quickly separate them, adding to the semi-circle until there are enough chairs for everybody here and any latecomers. Then I make a big point of introducing myself to Alice.

'I'm Fern. I've just moved here. I'm married to Drew, the new doctor.'

I hold out my hand in a strong and confident fashion and stare into Alice's eyes, telling myself not to break eye contact or offer a weak handshake when the moment comes, even if the touch of her skin will make my own start to crawl.

'It's lovely to meet you. I'm Alice.'

We shake. We smile. We both do a great acting job.

And now we're officially friends.

Yeah, right.

'I think I met your husband in the pub the other night. Rory, was it? He seems like a really nice guy.'

The kind of guy who doesn't deserve what you did to him behind his back.

'Oh yes, he said he met another couple from Manchester. He told me you were nice. You and your husband.'

You already know how nice my husband is.

'It's so good to meet you. I've been looking forward to it, actually. Although I must admit that I've been a little nervous.'

'Nervous? Why?'

Alice looks so awkward as she waits to hear what I'm going to say, and I just love it.

'Well, I was hoping we might be friends. See, I don't know anybody here, and I don't mean to be rude, but you might be the only person who is a similar age to me.'

That is a slight exaggeration because while this village is small, there are people of all ages here. But I kept my voice low for that last part so as not to offend any of the other women around us if they overheard, but it also has the added benefit of making Alice feel like I'm already letting her in on a little secret we can share. I'm determined to befriend this woman and make her feel as bad as possible because she deserves to feel guilty. So far, it's going well.

'Oh, I see,' Alice replies with a little chuckle. 'I'm sure we can be friends. You seem lovely.'

I do, don't I? But appearances can be deceptive. I know that better than anyone.

'Have you been doing this for a while?' I ask Alice, gesturing to all the chairs and cups.

'Yes, ever since I got to the village.'

'When was that?'

'About six months ago.'

Her reference to the timeline of when her affair with my husband ended forces me to grit my teeth before I ask another question.

'Why did you move here?'

'It was my husband's idea, he grew up in the village.'

'I see. And you were happy to just move?'

'Yeah, I thought it was a good opportunity.'

A good opportunity to end your affair before it got exposed, more like.

'Sorry, if you could just excuse me for a minute,' Alice says, very much ready to eject herself from this situation. 'I need to help out over there.'

She smiles before scurrying away over to the table, where she picks up a packet of biscuits and gets to work laying them out on plates. It's nothing that Audrey and the rest of the gang couldn't have managed with, and it's obvious Alice was just eager to stop talking to me. But she won't get away from me that easily. I'm going to be here all morning, and I'm sure we'll get the chance to speak again. I do hope so because we have plenty to talk about. But for now, I'll just go and make some small talk with a few of the other women here.

Women who have genuine smiles and honourable intentions.

Women that don't lie or give vague answers.

Women that have nothing to hide.

I used to be one of those women once. But things change. Now I'm just like Alice with all my secrets and ulterior motives. But there is still one big difference between me and her.

She thinks she has already won.

I, on the other hand, know that the game is still very much in play.

TEN

DREW

My bad mood from yesterday has carried over into today, but not just because Alice failed to reply to my message last night. It's because I'm having great difficulty getting my computer to do what it's supposed to be doing. No matter how many times I click my mouse, tap on the keyboard or give the monitor a nudge, nothing seems to be working.

The internet connection here seems to be terrible.

Welcome to life in the middle of nowhere, I guess.

'Julie, please could you come and take a look at this?' I say through the phone to my receptionist, after I've spent the last ten minutes trying and failing to send a single email.

Julie appears quickly to offer some assistance, but all she ends up doing is trying all the things I've already tried, and it's obvious that neither of us are IT experts.

'We sometimes have problems with the internet if there's bad weather in the area,' she tells me after it becomes clear that nothing is working for us.

'So, it's going to be like this every time it rains?'

'Erm.'

'I mean, it rained a lot in Manchester, but things still worked.'

'I understand. I think it has to do with the signal strength too. It's not very good here.'

'How are people supposed to get anything done?'

'I can call somebody out to take a look at it. Although it usually gets better once the weather clears up, and it's looking nice this afternoon.'

'Fine, whatever,' I reply in a huff before telling Julie to send in the next patient, because there's not much else that I can do in here without access to my network.

I feel bad for being curt with my receptionist because she's clearly a pleasant woman who is trying her best, but this is just one problem too many. I could handle the archaic internet connection if everything else was going well in my life, but it's not, so this is almost the final straw.

The knock on my door forces me to snap out of my pity party and put my professional face on as I prepare to welcome in another patient. Then I see who it is, and it's almost impossible for me to not look surprised.

'Hi, Drew, how's it going?' Rory says, taking a seat in the chair beside my desk. 'Settling in okay?'

I can only hope that Alice's husband is here for medical reasons and not because he knows about the conversation his wife and I had in this very same room yesterday.

'Oh, hey, Rory. Yeah, settling in just fine, thank you. Is everything okay with you?'

'Not exactly. I've been having a few issues, unfortunately.'

With your health or your wife?

'I see. What seems to be the problem?' I ask nervously. I'm fiddling with the lid to one of my pens, although I also notice that Rory is fiddling with his wedding ring on his finger, and it's clear he's just as awkward here as I am. Or maybe he's just plain worried based on what he tells me next.

'It started about a month ago. I noticed I was losing a bit of weight, even though I wasn't exercising or eating anything less. I've kept an eye on it, but the weight still seems to be coming off. I mean, don't get me wrong, I could have done with losing a few inches around my waist, but this is more than that. At this rate, I'll have a six pack by Easter.'

Unexplained weight loss is always a troubling symptom and one that warrants immediate investigation, but as I've been trained to do, I make sure not to display my concern in any way so as to keep the patient calm and reassured.

'I see. What about your appetite? Has that changed?'

'I didn't think it had, but my wife noticed in the past week or so that I've not been eating as much as usual. Leaving left-overs where there usually weren't any. Not suggesting take-aways on a weekend like I did previously. That kind of thing.'

'Okay,' I say, processing the answers while trying not to imagine him curled up on the sofa with Alice at a weekend, enjoying a pizza or a curry, because I wish that was me, not him. 'Any other issues? Have you been going to the toilet more or less than usual?'

'I'd say less than usual.'

Another red flag, but I give nothing away.

'Do you have any pain anywhere?'

'Not that I've noticed. I've had a few bad headaches recently though.'

'Okay. Anything else?'

'I think that's it.'

'I see. Well, let's have a quick look at you then. I'll check your blood pressure first.'

I quickly set up the sphygmomanometer, or blood pressure monitor as it's known in layman's terms, and attach it to his bicep before checking the reading, while Rory looks around my sparsely decorated surgery. I don't have any personal items in here yet, but maybe I should add something, just to give the room a little more life. At the moment it's all health charts and sterilised equipment. I used to have a photo of Fern on my desk back in Manchester, although by the end I felt like it was only there to keep up appearances rather than because I wanted to see my wife's face while I worked. And funnily enough, that photo hasn't made it out of the box I packed it in when I left. Our marriage has changed so much in the last few years that old photos of us don't do it justice anymore. The smiles I made when posing for pictures were once genuine, but they stopped being that way, so much so that I can't remember the last time I really smiled around Fern. Actually, I can. It was when she said we could move here, but even that was only because I knew I'd be nearer to Alice again. Somehow, I don't think that quite counts.

'Everything looks okay there. Now, if you can just roll up your other sleeve for me, I'll just take some blood.'

Rory does as I say, and I carefully draw blood from him with my needle, something I've done countless times before, but it's an act that also requires great concentration so as not to cause the patient any pain.

'Okay, if you could just step on those scales for me over there and I'll check your weight.'

Rory again follows my command, and I'm enjoying the power dynamic that exists between us. Even if outside of this room, he still has the upper hand over me in terms of Alice.

'That's great, thank you,' I say once I've made a note of the numbers on the scales, even though I know it's not great, because I don't need to measure Rory's height to know that he is definitely on the underweight side.

'Do you have any history of cancer in your family?' I ask him, wishing there was some way I could put across that question without making it obvious what disease it is that I might be concerned about the most.

'Erm, I think so. I'd have to check, I'm not sure.'

'I see.'

'Is that what you think it might be?'

'No, not at all. I just have to ask.'

Rory nods nervously before I invite him to retake his seat.

'How many units of alcohol would you say you have per week?'

'Do people ever tell you the truth when you ask them that?'

'I hope so.'

'Considering you met me in the pub, you already know I like a drink.'

'Just talk to me like a doctor, not a guy you had a pint with.'

Rory smiles before admitting he has twenty units, which I'm sure is a lie, but I write it down anyway. Then I ask him some more questions about his diet, and he answers them all while I scribble a few notes down.

'I thought you would just type them on the computer,' Rory says, noticing my rather old-fashioned way of doing things, but he understands once I tell him I'm having problems with the network today.

'Do you want me to take a look at it?' he offers, and I remember then that he works in IT, but I just thank him before politely declining. Somehow, it feels bad to have him do me a favour considering what I've done to him behind his back, so I tell him it's probably just interference from the weather, and he agrees.

'Yeah, that is a problem up here. If it carries on then let me know and I'll come down and take a look at it for you. Free of charge.'

Rory really is a nice guy, which doesn't make what has happened between his wife and I easier to think about, but I can't be put off by that. So what if he's a nice guy? I'm in love with Alice, and if she loved him, she wouldn't have got involved with me. And maybe he's only nice in public? Who knows what he's like behind closed doors? It certainly helps me to keep pursuing his wife if I think of Rory as a bad guy rather than a good one.

'What happens now?' Rory asks me once I've finished writing.

'I'll get your blood test sent off and let you know the results, if there's anything we need to look at further.'

'Do you think there will be?'

'Most likely not, but it's good to check to be on the safe side.'

'What do you think it could be?'

'It might be nothing.'

'But losing weight for no reason is not good, right?'

'It doesn't mean it's anything serious. We'll run a few tests just to be sure.'

'So, what happens now?' Rory persists, probably just anxious.

'Like I said, we'll run the blood test, and I'll give you a call with the results. In the meantime, monitor your symptoms and come and see me if anything changes. Apart from that, you're good to go.'

'Thanks,' Rory says, and he pulls down his shirt sleeve and fiddles with the button on it. 'I'm sure it's nothing, but I thought I'd come just in case. I guess health's important, isn't it?'

'If it wasn't then I'd be out of a job.'

Rory laughs at my joke, and I'm glad I've been able to put him at ease, for a few moments at least. I'm also proud of myself for acting professionally despite my secret history with this man. Maybe I can be mature about all of this after all. But I can't resist asking him about Alice in one form or another.

'Have you told your wife that you were coming here today?'

'No. I didn't want to worry her. Should I have?'

'No, best not to. Like you say, no point worrying her.'

I'm glad Alice has no idea that her husband has been to see me and is now officially under my care.

Rory gets up to leave then, and I decide to walk him over to the door, just to be friendly and ensure he leaves here a little less anxious than when he arrived.

'You have a good day,' I say to him as I open the door, but just before I go, he asks me if I'll be in the pub this weekend because he'd like to buy me a pint.

'Possibly,' I say. 'And thank you, that would be very kind.'

Rory leaves then, and I give him a wave goodbye before glancing into the waiting room and seeing that all the chairs in there are empty. That means I've got some time before my next appointment, so I close the door and go back to my desk.

I check the computer again and see that the internet connection does seem to have been restored, which is good news and means I can type up my report from my latest patient. I can also record that I have taken a blood sample and will be sending it off for testing. But I hesitate before typing anything on the server, and as I look down at the vial of blood lying beside my keyboard, I have a thought. It's a thought that I shouldn't be having in my professional capacity, but it's one I can't ignore now that it has come to me so strongly.

What if I didn't ask for the blood test? What if I just tossed this vial away so that nothing would happen? What if I just rang Rory in a week or so and told him that everything was fine?

That would be risky and dangerous if, as I suspect, there is something sinister going on in Rory's body that warrants further attention. It would also be taking a very big chance with a guy who came to me today for help. If he does have something wrong with him, and some of his symptoms suggest he does, then he needs medical care sooner rather than later. So why am I thinking about delaying it? Why am I giving thought to the idea of potentially reducing the odds of him being okay, if it does turn out that he is seriously ill?

I know why. *Alice.* I want her so much that I'd be willing to risk her husband's life to have her. Is it such a bad thing if Rory might have a life-threatening condition? It wouldn't be the worst thing in the world if he wasn't around anymore, would it?

Picking up the vial, I stare at the red liquid inside before making my decision. Then I put it inside the pocket of my suit jacket, where I plan to carry it home before disposing of it in the bin. That's the best place for it now, or at least it's the best place to ensure that if Rory is ill, help won't be coming his way anytime soon.

ELEVEN

FERN

The coffee morning has been pleasant, if not a little dull. There wasn't really an agenda after we had all taken our seats in the semi-circle and started to sip from our cups of tea. Instead, it just seemed to be about striking up a conversation with the person next to you, and while I managed to do that easily enough, the people seated on either side of me weren't exactly filled with the kinds of stories that could be classed as 'entertaining'.

The lady to my left, Agatha, was the type of person who could find the negative in any situation, and she spent twenty minutes moaning about how she had spent an awfully long time waiting for a builder to come and look at her plans for a potential garage conversion, before being shocked at the quote he gave her for the work that was required. Then she lamented the weather, the state of the road surface on her street, as well as throwing in her dismay at the prime minister's recent policies just for good measure. Five more minutes of listening to her would have had me reaching for a bottle of vodka rather than another cup of tea, so I found a way to strike up a conversation with the woman to my right instead, although that hadn't gone much better.

She was a little cheerier, but she was also slightly loopy, in the nicest sense of the word. She'd burst out laughing after everything she said, regardless of whether or not it was meant to be funny, before she would go very quiet and not say anything for a few minutes. It made her quite difficult to talk to as I couldn't tell if she was enjoying our chat or hating it. I got my answer when I'd just finished telling her all about my recent house move only to notice that she had fallen asleep at some point during my story and had missed everything I'd just said.

But of course, I didn't come here for conversation or to make friends, not really. I came here to get closer to my love rival. Unfortunately, the seating arrangements made that a little difficult.

Alice was seated on the opposite side of the semi-circle to me, and despite looking in her direction several times, she did a very good job of not making eye contact. She just kept her attention on the people beside her, chatting away, chomping on a few chocolate biscuits and getting up once to bring another pot of tea over for the group.

I'd made sure to thank her as she had refilled my cup, and she had smiled at me before quickly moving on to Sleeping Beauty beside me, but as far as our interactions had gone in the meeting that was as far as it went. In the end, I'm relieved when the hour is up, and as a few people start to drift away out of the room, I make sure to catch up with Alice again before she can leave too.

I catch her over by the table tidying up a few of the dirty teacups and, as I say hi again, she flinches a little as she realises I'm right beside her.

'So, that was interesting,' I say with a wry smile. 'I think I'm going to have to work on my conversational skills. The woman beside me fell asleep in the middle of one of my stories.'

'Oh, that's just Barbara, she's always dozing.'

Alice knocks over one of the cups in her haste and spills tea all over the tablecloth, making more of a mess than before she started cleaning up.

'Don't worry, I've got it,' I say, and I pick up the upended cup before making sure the spilt tea isn't running down onto the floor.

'Sorry, I'm just a little tired myself,' Alice admits. 'I didn't sleep well last night.'

'Oh, any reason?'

'Erm, no. Just a bad night, I think.'

Alice carries on moving cups around, stacking them on to a tray, which I presume she will carry out of here into the kitchen at the back of the room.

'Well, thank you for coming,' Alice says to me before looking to leave with her tray, but I don't let her get away that easily.

'I'll help you with the washing up if you'd like,' I offer.

'It's okay, there's a dishwasher back there.'

'Then I'll help you put the cups into it.'

Alice must know she can't keep turning down my offers of help without seeming weird or, at worst, rude, so she reluctantly agrees, and I follow her into the kitchen as the rest of the attendees file out of the room.

'If you don't mind me asking, why do you help out here?' I say to Alice as we begin to load the dishwasher. 'I mean, it's not quite the place I'd expect someone like you to be hanging around.'

'Someone like me?'

'I mean, you're much younger than everyone else and glamorous, if you don't mind me saying. I'd have thought tea and biscuits with some old ladies would hardly be your scene.'

'I like it here. Everyone's nice.'

'Yeah, they are. But I'm guessing you volunteer, so you don't have to do it, do you?'

'No, I suppose not. But I don't work, so it's nice to keep busy and help out. Community is a big thing around here.'

'I can see that. Well, maybe I'll have to get more involved. We could organise some things together, if you like?'

I'm trying too hard. Being overly keen. A little desperate. Clingy, even. But all of it is making the woman beside me squirm, so there's not a chance in hell that I'll ease off.

Alice looks very uncomfortable at my suggestion and doesn't say anything as she turns the dishwasher on and wipes down the countertop.

'Thank you for helping. I can finish up the rest myself,' she tells me.

'Don't be silly, you've still got the chairs to do,' I remind her, and I go back into the main hall, where I start stacking the seats we just used for the meeting.

Alice must be wishing that I would just leave her alone, but I'm enjoying making her squirm, and as she reluctantly comes to help me, I have another idea of how to make her feel even worse about what she has done with my husband in the past.

'You know, a cup of tea is lovely, but how about a proper drink?' I say breezily. 'We could go to the pub for lunch. How about it?'

Alice drops the chair she is holding, and it clatters loudly on the floor of this otherwise empty hall.

'Are you okay?' I ask her, feigning concern.

'Yeah, it just slipped. Sorry.'

She picks the chair back up and carries it over to the stack, where I'm standing.

'Here, let me help you with that,' I say, taking it from her and adding it to the pile.

'I think that's it,' Alice says, looking around at the tidy hall.

'Looks like it. So how about that drink?'

'Oh, erm. I can't.'

'Are you sure?'

I couldn't fake any more disappointment if I tried. When are the nominations announced for the Oscars again?

'Erm, I have a few things to do,' Alice says, possibly doing just as good an acting job in her own way.

'It's just one drink. We don't have to get lunch.'

'Sorry.'

'What have you got to do?'

'Erm... just a few errands to run.'

'Like what?'

'Erm...'

I'm enjoying watching Alice scramble for an excuse to get out of going to the pub with me, and it's interesting to see just how bad she is at lying. She must think I'm incredibly nosey for asking so many questions, but I'm having too much fun toying with her to stop enquiring.

'I need to go to the post office. And I have to go and do some shopping for tonight's dinner,' she eventually tells me, and I guess it's a valid answer, though it took a long time for her to come up with it.

'Oh, okay. That's a shame. We'll have to do it some other time then.'

'Yeah, some other time.'

Alice grabs her coat then and heads for the door, and I follow her, putting on my own coat and carrying my umbrella.

It's still raining as we step outside, and I notice then that Alice doesn't have an umbrella of her own, giving me another chance to make her uncomfortable around me.

'Where are you going? I could walk with you if you'd like, and we could share this?' I say, holding up my umbrella.

'No, it's okay, I'll be fine, thank you,' she says, keeping her distance from me as the raindrops start to hit her coat. 'I better get going. Nice to see you again.'

With that, Alice turns and leaves as quickly as she can, but she isn't looking where she is going and she steps in a big puddle, splashing water all up her legs as she goes.

'Are you okay?' I call after her, but she just waves me off and keeps going, hurrying away until she makes it around the street corner and disappears from view.

I stay standing there for a moment outside the church hall, as the rain hammers down on the umbrella above my head, and think about what just occurred. Alice clearly did not like being around me, and who can blame her? I can't say I enjoyed being around her either because it's hard work not giving in to my strongest desire, which is to punch her in that pretty little face. But I'm not the bad guy here, she is, along with Drew, so I'm not going to let the awkwardness of it all deter me. I wasn't able to get her to go for a drink with me, but I have another idea as to how to make her squirm, and it's even better than the pub idea.

I can't wait for Drew to come home so I can tell him all about it.

TWELVE

DREW

I've seen five more patients since Rory came into my surgery, but unlike with him I have followed all the protocols. Any tests that needed to be done have been applied for, and any medication that needs to be administered has been prescribed, so it's the one vial of blood in my suit jacket that is the only evidence of my malpractice so far.

Even though the end of the working day beckons, I'm well aware that it's not too late for me to change my mind, remove the blood sample from my pocket and process it, so it can be sent for testing. Nobody will know that I had a brief lapse of morals, and Rory will get the test results he deserves. Or I could just leave it where it is and carry on as if I've done nothing wrong, hoping that my conscience won't bother me too much in the days that are to follow.

The fact that the blood remains in my possession and is not already on its way to be delivered elsewhere is proof that, despite my misgivings, I haven't gone back on my dark deed. By the time Julie tells me that the practice is closed and we're done for the day, there is no way I'm going back now. All I have to do is keep calm as I take the sample home and then dispose of it there, and then it's over. But before I put my jacket on and leave, I decide to send another message to Alice.

She still hasn't responded to my first one, but I know she's read it. At least she isn't ignoring me completely then, and that thought gives me the courage to try one more time.

> *Hi. I hope you've had a good day. We still need to talk. Will you meet me on the beach tonight at 8 p.m.? Near the lifeguard sign? Tell Rory you're just going for a walk or something. I'll tell Fern the same. I really need to see you. Drew x*

I'm happy with what I've written, so I press send and hope for the best. To my surprise, I get a response almost immediately.

> *Okay. I'll be there. I need to talk to you too.*

Great, she's agreed to meet me. Okay, so there's no kiss or any kind of affection at the end of her message, but this will do for now. It's a start. She's willing to talk. It's only a minor thing, but I can instantly feel the dark cloud that has been hanging over me lift. Suddenly, life doesn't seem so bleak after all.

> *Thank you. I can't wait to see you x*

I wonder if she'll reply to that, but she doesn't. No matter, I got what I wanted. A meeting. Now all I have to do is make sure it goes well.

I leave the practice and wave goodbye to Julie, though I'm careful not to make too much of a sudden movement in case it causes the blood sample to fall from my jacket pocket as I go. I feel better about it once I'm in my car and start driving, and by the time I get home, I'm certain I'll get away with what I'm doing. I just need to make sure Fern doesn't see me with the blood, but she's in the shower when I get back, so I take my chance to dispose of the evidence.

Putting the vial over the sink, I open it up and pour the contents down the plughole before running the tap to ensure all the red liquid has run away. Then I put the vial in the bin, burying it beneath some of the waste already in there and, once that is done, I remove the rubbish bag and take it outside, where I drop it in the bin and figure out how long it is until it's due to be collected. The binmen should come tomorrow so that will be perfect. Now all I have to do is go back inside and act like I didn't just do something that the younger, innocent doctor I used to be would have been horrified at. Then again, that's not the kind of doctor I have been for a while now, long before I came to this village and added another black mark to my professional record.

I pour myself a glass of wine and take a seat at the table, hearing the creak of the wicker chair that holds my weary body as I wait for Fern to finish her shower and come downstairs. This gives me the time that I need to process my actions and justify them in my head a little more.

Rory is probably fine. What I've just done won't make a difference in the grand scheme of things. And if he is ill, it's probably too late anyway.

Feeling better, but perhaps only because of the wine, I pour myself another glass before Fern makes an appearance and asks me how my day was.

'Fine. No dramas,' I tell her. 'What about yours? Did you go into the village?'

'I did, actually,' she says, noting my drink and fixing one for herself before joining me at the table. 'I went to the coffee meetup at the church hall.'

'How was it?'

'It was okay. Kind of what I expected it to be.'

'Did you make any friends?'

'One, actually. Alice, Rory's partner.'

I swallow hard before grinning uneasily. I knew they would run into each other at some point. *Stay cool, Drew.*

'That's great. Good to hear.'

'Yeah, she's lovely. We had a nice chat. I helped her tidy up at the end.'

'Good. Very good.'

I'm reaching for the wine bottle again, my hands shaking slightly as I think about the ramifications of Fern becoming friends with Alice. I'd presumed, or rather hoped, that Alice would be sensible enough to keep her distance from my wife, but maybe that's easier said than done, if Fern is desperate to make a friend. My wife must be doing all the legwork in the budding relationship while my ex-mistress just has to grin and bear it, much like I am doing right here.

'Yeah, I think we might become good friends.'

'You do?'

My hand is shaking as I pour another measure for myself.

'Yeah, why not? I mean, we're a similar age. Both come from the same place. Both ended up living here. I think it would be weird if we didn't become friends, don't you?'

'I don't know. Just because you have a few things in common, it doesn't mean you're going to get along.'

'I suppose. I guess time will tell. I was thinking, to maybe help things along, I could invite her over for dinner. Rory as well. What do you think?'

The wine bottle slips out of my hand, and despite my best efforts, I can't quite catch it in time, and it rolls off the table before smashing on the floor, creating a red mess on the white tiles, a mess so vivid in its colour that it is not too dissimilar to the blood that was in the sink a moment ago.

'What are you doing?' Fern cries as she jumps up and rushes to get the kitchen roll.

'Wait. Be careful. I'll do it,' I say as I take over, not wanting her to risk cutting herself on the broken glass.

'How did that happen?'

'I don't know. It just slipped.'

I wasn't planning on creating such a mess, but at least it's stopped Fern from talking about inviting Alice and Rory over. By the time I have cleaned up, I'm hoping she might have forgotten about what she said. But no such luck.

'So, what do you think?'

'About what?'

'About asking Alice and Rory here for dinner? I could cook them a nice meal, we could have some wine. Hopefully you won't drop the bottle on the floor this time.'

She's joking, but I can't laugh because none of what she has just said is funny. The thought of both Alice and Rory in this house, sitting around the dinner table with Fern, is my idea of hell. Not only would it be incredibly awkward for both me and Alice, but it would require both of us to do some serious acting to pretend like everything was okay, and I'm not sure we're capable of it. Maybe we are, but I wouldn't want to take that chance, not when the stakes are so high.

'I don't know. We've only just moved in. We've barely had time to settle. I think it's a bit early to start planning dinner parties.'

'I'm just trying to help us make friends here. We don't know anybody.'

'It's still early days. We've got all the time in the world. And if you want to socialise with people, there's a perfectly good pub in the village for that. We can eat and drink until we're merry there but without all the hassle of hosting and tidying up afterwards.'

'I don't understand why you wouldn't want them here. Is there something wrong?'

'No, of course not.'

Damn it, I can't think of another way to get Fern to drop this without it seeming weird.

'Then why can't I invite them?'

'Fine. You can invite them. But not yet, okay?'

'Why not?'

Then I have it. An excuse not to have them here yet.

'Because Rory came to see me today, and I think there might be something wrong.'

'What?'

I shouldn't really be talking about this kind of thing, but needs must.

'He came for a check-up today. I can't tell you anything more, but I'm not sure a dinner party is what he needs right now.'

'Is he going to be okay?'

'Yeah, I'm sure he'll be fine. But he seemed a little stressed. Very distracted, which is understandable. But I think he'll hardly make great company at the moment. So maybe let's put the plans for an invite on hold for now, okay?'

I'm relieved when Fern takes that as a good enough reason to drop the idea, and with that potential disaster of a dinner party averted for at least a little while, I offer to help make dinner. Fern accepts, and we work together to cook some chicken and rice with a few vegetables before we sit down to eat. I make sure to keep checking my watch because I have my date with Alice to come, and I wouldn't want to risk being late.

Once the meal is over with and I've cleaned up, Fern suggests we watch a movie, but I have other ideas.

'I was thinking of going for a walk tonight.'

'Oh okay, I'll come with you. Where are we going?'

Damn it.

'Erm, well, it's less of a walk and more of a jog, actually.'

'A jog? Since when do you jog?'

'I've been meaning to start. I need to get more active. I can hardly be telling my patients to get more exercise if I don't look like I follow my own advice.'

'But you hate exercise.'

'That's not true.'

'Yes, it is. You told me that it's not as important as other medical professionals make it out to be. Remember? You said it's all just luck whether we get ill or not, and no amount of running or lifting weights or eating salads will change that.'

'I don't think I was quite that blunt.'

'You were.'

'Well, maybe I was wrong. I can change my mind about it all, can't I? I mean, all that stuff obviously is important.'

'So, where are you going to jog?'

'I don't know. Maybe into the village. Or down along the beach, perhaps.'

'Be careful. It's dark out there.'

'I'll be fine.'

I head upstairs to change into my shorts and T-shirt and move quickly, because I'm afraid Fern might offer to come jogging with me. She is right, I hate exercise and have never been the most active of people, although part of that is down to the fact that I've always had a fast metabolism, so unwanted weight gain has never really been a problem for me.

Sure, she might be suspicious of my desire to go out for a run, but it's a legitimate reason for me to leave the house for a little while, and that's all I need. I'm not sure how long I'm going to be with Alice at the beach, but I'm willing to be there for as long as it takes. And, who knows, if we get physical out there then at least I'll be able to come back looking a little sweaty, and Fern will really believe I just went for a run.

Perfect.

THIRTEEN

FERN

My husband is 'going for a jog'.

Yeah right. And pigs might fly.

I don't believe a word Drew has said to me about wanting to get some exercise this evening, and even though he looks the part in his T-shirt, shorts and trainers as he stands by the door and prepares to leave, I suspect the only physical exertion he has on his mind involves that woman.

He must be going to see Alice. So be it.

Although there's only one way for me to find out.

I wave him goodbye as he disappears out the front door before springing into action, grabbing my shoes and putting on my coat before peering outside to see how far he has got.

I can see the shape of him out there in the darkness. He's just turned left out of our driveway and is now walking down the street. Walking, not running. Not even making the effort to keep up with his lie. He must think I'm so stupid.

I wait a few more seconds before opening the front door and creeping outside, closing it carefully behind me so as not to make a sound and tip Drew off that I'm following him. Then I set off in the same direction he went in, keeping a safe distance but not losing sight of him as he walks ahead of me.

I tail him down the street and around the bend before he makes a move towards the beach. I see him glance back over his shoulder at one point, but I duck down behind a parked car and keep my presence a secret, and once I'm back on the trail, I see that he is now down on the sand.

So, he's meeting her at the beach, is he? A little rendezvous by the water underneath the stars?

How romantic.

How disgusting.

I decide not to follow him directly down onto the beach due to the lack of places to hide should he turn around and look back again, so I stay up on the road but keep him within view. When he eventually stops, I see him standing beside the lifeguard sign, and I guess that is the landmark where Alice will know to find him.

But where is she?

Ten minutes pass, and there is no sign of her, and I wonder if my husband has been stood up. He looks so pathetic over there by himself, supposedly out running yet just statically standing by the sign, looking around for some company. Eventually, he gets it.

I see the flash of blonde in the moonlight and know it is her, even though I can't quite see her face yet. I also recognise that confident gait, and I keep my eyes on Alice as she gets closer to Drew before they are finally together again.

Now that they are, will they hug? Kiss? Start rolling around on the sand together? No, they don't do any of that, even though it appears that Drew is more than eager to bridge the gap between them. Alice seems a little more tentative, and as I watch them start talking, I really wish I could hear what they are saying. Alas, there is no way I can get any closer to them without giving myself away, so I stay where I am and make do with maintaining a visual on them.

Their conversation goes on for a while and, at one point, it seems to get a little heated, if Drew throwing his hands up in the air in exasperation is anything to go by. He's shouting a little now too, but I still can't make out the words, which is very frustrating. I am pleased by the fact that it seems like all might not be well in the world of these two little lovebirds, and it certainly seems that way as the meeting ends without either of them embracing.

Alice turns to leave, and while Drew tries to make her stay, she brushes him off and makes her exit, leaving him once again alone on the beach.

Wow. I wasn't expecting that. Is the affair over now? Did Drew move here thinking he could just pick up where they left off, only to find that Alice has other ideas? If so, it seems she has changed while my husband has not. If that's the case, then I guess Rory is lucky because his wife might just love him after all. But my partner is clearly still as much of a rotten scoundrel as he was before we moved here, and with that now as clear as day to me, I'll have to decide what I'm going to do about it.

First I need to get home before Drew does.

It turns out that at least one of us is going to get some exercise tonight after all because I have little choice but to start jogging down the street to ensure that I make it back to the house first. Like my husband, I've never been particularly active but I'm not totally unfit, and I manage to get home without being too out of breath. I am sweating a little though, so I quickly take off my shoes and coat before I go to the bathroom and splash some water on my face to cool down. Then I take my place on the sofa and turn the TV on, which is where I am when Drew arrives back fifteen minutes later, looking decidedly less sweaty than I was a moment ago.

'How was your run?' I ask him casually before turning my head back to the screen.

'Fine. I'm just going to have a shower.'

I hear him stomping up the stairs and rather noisily getting undressed before he shuts the bathroom door and turns the water on. He's definitely in a bad mood. Just like the one he was in yesterday. I wonder if that was the first time he got the hint that Alice might not be as receptive to his charms as she once was before.

There's trouble in paradise.

I try and concentrate on the TV while I wait for him to join me, but he doesn't come back downstairs after his shower, and I end up having to go up to find him. When I do, he's already in bed, lying under the duvet and looking at something on his phone.

'What are you doing?' I ask him as he lowers his phone when he sees me walk in.

'Nothing. I'm just tired after my run. Needed a bit of a lie down.'

'You didn't overdo it, did you?'

'No, I'm fine. Just chilling out.'

'Is everything okay?'

'Yeah, why wouldn't it be?'

'You seemed a bit moody when you got back.'

'Did I?'

'Yeah.'

Drew shrugs before telling me again that he's fine.

'Okay. I might have an early night too, actually.'

I quickly go around the house turning off the lights before joining him in bed. Even though he is saying noth-ing, I can sense the despair coming off him. He must be feeling like an idiot for coming here for Alice only to be shunned by her. The question is, what is he going to do about it?

'I've been thinking, maybe I'm not cut out for village life after all,' he confesses to me out of the blue a few minutes later.

'What?'

'It's just very quiet here, isn't it?'

'What did you expect?'

'I don't know. It's just been a bit of a culture change.'

'Don't you like it?'

'I'm not sure. Do you?'

'It's okay.'

'Yeah...'

Drew's voice drifts off, but I keep the conversation going.

'What are you saying? You want to leave? Go back to Manchester?'

'I don't know.'

'You do realise it was your idea to come here.'

'I know it was.'

'I was happy to stay there. You're the one who made us move. We wouldn't be here if it wasn't for you.'

'Okay, calm down.'

'I'm just struggling to understand how you could suddenly change your mind. You couldn't have been happier when we got here. What's happened since then?'

'Nothing.'

'Are you telling me the truth?'

'Yes.'

Another opportunity for my husband to come clean to me. Yet another lie that has come out of his mouth.

'If something has happened, anything at all, you can tell me,' I say, giving him yet another chance to do the right thing. 'I'm your wife. You can be honest with me.'

Ha. The absurdity of it almost makes me laugh, but I keep in character.

'Nothing's happened,' Drew lies again. 'I'm just thinking out loud. But I'm happy here. Honestly, I am.'

I guess he's decided not to give up on Alice yet then. It looks like we're staying. More importantly, it looks like he's not going to take the chance to quit while he's already behind.

'There's a village fete on Saturday,' I tell him as we turn off the lights and sink down deeper onto our pillows. 'Maybe we could go and check it out. It might be fun.'

'Sure,' Drew replies before rolling over and turning his back to me.

I stare at his torso in the darkness until I hear his soft snores, before I roll over myself and try and get some rest. But it's difficult when all I can think about is how my husband is still the same man he was when he started his affair.

Maybe there is a chance for Alice to avoid my wrath, but Drew? He deserves it. That much is clear. Agreeing to move here was a test, and he's failed it miserably. It doesn't matter that his mistress seems to have had her fill of him.

I'm not done with him yet.

Not by a long way.

FOURTEEN

DREW

It's always nice when the sun shines on the weekend, and the sky is a perfect blue as Fern and I leave the house and head in the direction of the village fete, which should be starting right about now. From what Fern has told me about it, there are going to be plenty of stalls offering food and drink, as well as various items available for sale, like candles and other nonsense that nobody needs but will most likely buy. Apparently, there is some live music on too, which should help the atmosphere, as well as a beer tent, which I'm keen to explore, and as I walk beside my wife in the direction of the music, I could almost be forgiven for thinking that this is going to be an enjoyable Saturday.

Almost.

Thoughts of Alice are never far from my mind and, if I'm honest, the only reason I am really going to this fete today is in the hopes that I might see her there. I won't be able to do much if she is there, not with Fern and most likely Rory around too, but just seeing her will be something. I miss her so much, and the words she said to me at the beach the other night are still ringing in my ears, replaying over and over again as I try to make some sense of them.

The meeting with Alice did not go well at all. I was glad when she turned up at the agreed time and place, but that was about as good as it got because she then proceeded to double down on what she had already told me during our first meeting in my surgery.

I came here to get away from you.

I'm trying to make a go of my marriage.

Leave me alone.

We're over.

I tried every trick in the book to get her to change her mind, from begging to even threatening to tell her husband what happened between us anyway. The only thing I didn't do was tell her about Rory's consultation with me and about my suspicions that he has something seriously wrong with him. I almost did, but I decided to keep that to myself for the time being, especially after what I did with the blood test. If the situation doesn't improve for me then I'm not afraid to play that card, using the idea of her being married to a sick man to potentially get her to see the error of her ways and choose me after all. That would be breaking the bounds of doctor–patient confidentiality, but to hell with that when there's so much more at stake for me here.

Considering how quiet and almost lifeless this village has been ever since I got here, it's quite a shock to see it so busy, once we make it to the fete and see just how many people have come out for it. There must be a couple of hundred people here. I'm sure there must be a few tourists as well, and all of them are mingling around the various stalls as a musician plays his guitar on a big stage in front of it all.

'This looks amazing,' Fern says before immediately being drawn over to a stall that is selling decorative chopping boards.

I linger behind her as she browses, detecting a strong scent of fried onions coming from one of the many stalls covered in red and blue bunting, while scanning the crowd for any sign of Alice, even though I know trying to spot her in such a busy place like this will be like trying to find a needle in a haystack. It's hard not to feel like today is going to be yet another disappointment in a long line of them.

'What do you think about this one for our kitchen?' Fern asks me, holding up a chopping board with the shape of a rose carved into it.

'Yeah, it's okay,' I say with a shrug. I'm really not interested. But I am interested when Fern tells me how much it will cost to buy it.

'Fifty pounds!' I exclaim, a little louder than I had planned to, and I notice the grumpy expression from the woman behind the stall who obviously feels like her items are fairly priced.

'Don't be a scrooge, we have to support local businesses,' my wife tells me before ordering me to get my wallet out and hand over the cash.

I do as I'm told though I'm still not happy about it, particularly because the stall owner now has a big smile on her face after receiving my money, which makes me think she might have just scammed us after all.

We wander on through the crowds, although I'm pleased to see that Fern has no interest in spending any more of my hard-earned money on things we don't need. We certainly could do with a drink, and by the time we reach the beer tent, I'm eager to join the back of the queue for the bar. But just before we do, we receive another warm welcome to the village, this time from Pat and his wife, Sheila; Pat tells me he runs the local butchers and that I'll have to come in and get my sausages from him now that I'm living nearby.

I promise him that I will before answering a few of his questions about what it's like to be a doctor, before I finally break away to buy myself a drink and quench my thirst. One beer quickly becomes two, and though I still have much on my mind, I'm starting to loosen up a little bit, my mood helped by not just the alcohol but the potent combination of the sunshine and the boisterous atmosphere here. Fern is having fun too and is talking to a couple who look only a little older than us, so I'm hoping she will latch on to them and be more interested in inviting them for dinner, in the process forgetting all about Alice and Rory.

And then I see them. Walking hand in hand over by the cake stall. Him saying something to her and her laughing in response. They look happy. Content. Like a proper married couple.

I feel sick just watching them, but they haven't seen me over here, so I'm able to keep punishing myself by tracking them as they move through the crowd. It's only as they get nearer that I realise they must be heading for the beer tent, the same one I am standing in, and suddenly I've left it too late to get out of the way before they catch me staring.

'Hey, Drew. How's it going?' Rory asks me, holding out his hand to greet me.

'Oh, hi, Rory. I'm good thanks, how are you?'

We shake as Alice and I make eye contact, but she quickly looks down and clearly has no interest in staying around to chat. Unfortunately for her, her husband does.

'Not a bad way to cap off your first week here, is it?' Rory says, gesturing around at all the activity we're surrounded by.

'No, I can't complain,' I say before looking back at Alice, who is still choosing to avoid me.

'That beer looks good. I might get one myself,' Rory says. 'Do you want a drink?'

He looks at his wife, and she shakes her head but looks like she quickly regrets it when Rory tells her he will go to the bar and meet her back here. Then he leaves her alone with me and, while she might not like it, I seize my chance.

'You look great,' I tell her, while careful to check that Fern is still preoccupied with the other couple and can't hear us.

'Thanks,' Alice mumbles back, barely audible over the music from the stage.

'You know, you don't have to be so cold to me. I think I deserve better than this.'

'I'm not being cold.'

'You're barely looking at me.'

That's an understatement. Alice's eyes are on everyone else here but the person talking to her.

'I'm trying not to make it obvious.'

'Make what obvious?'

'That we have a past.'

'It's going to be more obvious if you keep acting like you can't stand me.'

'I'm not doing that.'

'Aren't you?'

The distance between us feels like a chasm.

'We just need to stay away from each other.'

'Why?'

'Because we do.'

'That doesn't make any sense. Fine, if you don't want me then I'll have to accept it. But we're going to be seeing a lot of each other because we live in a small village, so I can't help that.'

'That's not what I mean.'

'Then what do you mean?'

'You know what I mean.'

I have to think about it for a moment before I see what Alice is getting at. The way she is looking at me. Now I see it. She doesn't hate me, not at all. She just doesn't trust herself around me.

'You're still attracted to me,' I realise, and it's hard to conceal the joy that rises up from inside.

'I'm trying to do the right thing by Rory.'

'By denying yourself what you really want?'

'By being a better person. The person he married.'

'And making yourself unhappy in the process? That sounds stupid to me.'

'Better to be stupid than to be a cheat.'

'It's a little late for that.'

I give Alice a wry smile, but she doesn't return it.

'That queue went quicker than I thought it would. Cheers!'

I turn around and realise that Rory has re-joined us, now armed with a pint of beer and holding his plastic cup towards mine.

'Oh, cheers,' I reply, and we bump cups before he takes a thirsty gulp. Then Fern reappears, and I'm annoyed I won't get to continue my private conversation with Alice. I'm even more annoyed when Fern brings up the dinner invitation subject again.

'Lovely to see you guys! I was just saying to Drew the other night that we should have you over for a meal some time!'

'That would be wonderful,' Rory replies eagerly. 'We're ready when you are!'

'Hang on a minute,' I say, trying to curtail any plans for the time being, but Fern is way too eager, and she proves it by suggesting a dinner date at very short notice.

Tonight.

'I'm sure they already have plans this evening,' I say, and Alice agrees, saying she thinks they have something already in the diary. But Rory isn't as convinced.

'I'm pretty sure we're free tonight,' Rory tells us before checking with Alice, but she obviously can't think of something to get us out of this mess.

'Great. Well, if you are free then we'd love to have you. How about eight o'clock?'

'We'll be there!' Rory says before he raises his beer to me

again. This time, I don't feel like bumping cups with him. Instead, I wish I could throw my drink in his face and get the hell out of here, because despite thinking that I was coming to this village to make my life more exciting again, so far, all I've managed to achieve is getting four people together in the same place who should have always been kept apart.

Tonight is going to be tricky, there's no doubt about it.

But I'll try and look on the bright side. It's a night with Alice, even if we're not alone.

That's better than nothing.

Right?

FIFTEEN

FERN

It's my first time hosting in my new home, so I'm a little nervous, but not just because I hope my guests enjoy the meal that I've cooked them. It's because this will be the first time I've been around Alice for a prolonged period of time and in a much more intimate setting than the coffee morning earlier in the week.

The butterflies in my stomach are making me edgy, but I doubt I'm feeling quite as anxious as my husband is. What must he be thinking now? Being forced to sit with his mistress and her husband at the dinner table, while I sit beside him and pretend like everything is fine? I'm surprised he's not been sick yet. Maybe he has. We got back from the fete a couple of hours ago, and I've barely seen him since.

'Is everything okay up there?' I ask him, calling up the stairs.

'No,' Drew shouts back, and I decide to go up to investigate. When I arrive in the bedroom, I find him lying on the bed with a wet flannel across his forehead.

'What's the matter?'

'I don't feel well.'

'Are you sick?'

'Maybe?'

I go to touch his face to check his temperature, but he moves away, so I can't.

'What's happened? You were fine at the fete.'

'I don't know. I've got a headache and feel a bit queasy. Maybe it was something I ate.'

'We've eaten the same things today, and I'm fine.'

'Maybe it's something else then.'

I frown at my husband, who is clearly faking sickness to try and get out of what would be a very uncomfortable dinner party for him. But like a parent who knows their child is playing games just to try and get out of a day at school, I have no patience for it.

'Well, you better get yourself up and feeling better because our guests will be arriving shortly,' I say, clapping my hands together and proving to him that I don't have time for this nonsense. But Drew doesn't give up that easily.

'I'm not sure I'm well enough for dinner,' he moans before touching his 'fevered' brow. 'We might have to cancel.'

'What? Are you serious?'

'I'm sorry, but it's not my fault that I'm ill.'

'I can't cancel now, it's too late. It's beyond last minute. They're probably already on their way. It'll be rude.'

'No, it won't be. There's still time.'

'I've made all the food. It's almost ready to go.'

'I'm sorry.'

'Well, I'm sorry too, but I'm not cancelling. We don't have any friends here yet and tonight is a perfect opportunity for us to make some, so I'm not going to miss it.'

'Are you kidding? I'd cancel if you were ill!'

'Would you? What about the party with the Harpers back in Manchester that time? I was throwing up all afternoon, and you still insisted on going.'

'It was a birthday party. It was different!'

'This is different too. It's our first chance to have friends in our new home, and I'm not going to miss it. Now, either you get up, get showered and come downstairs to join me, or I'll have to tell them that you're not well and you can stay up here. But I'm not cancelling.'

I stride out of the room then, not feeling at all in the least bit guilty about how unsympathetic I've just been to my husband's 'plight'. I know it's all just a façade, and he'll try anything to keep Alice away from me tonight. Too bad it's not going to work for him.

Back in the kitchen, I check on the food in the oven and see that it is almost ready, so I turn the temperature down a little bit and check the time. Our guests are due any minute. I wonder how Alice is feeling. Probably as sick as Drew, I imagine. I also wonder if she has tried pulling any last-minute stunts like faking illness and hoping her partner will cancel for her. I wouldn't put it past her. Both her and Drew are devious little souls. But I have a feeling that Rory is as eager to make new friends as I am, so hopefully he won't let her cancel either.

The knock on the front door five minutes later tells me the dinner date is still on, and I quickly take off my apron before washing my hands and taking a deep breath.

This is it.

Show time.

'Thank you so much for coming!' I cry as I throw open the front door and welcome in my guests with open arms.

'Thank you for having us,' Rory says as he greets me just as warmly, and I see he has brought a bottle of champagne for the occasion.

Alice is less enthusiastic about things as she lingers behind him, but I make sure to give her a big hug as she enters, squeezing her just enough to hopefully hurt her slightly, before I tell my guests to make themselves at home.

'Drew will be with us in just a minute,' I say. 'How about I pour us some drinks in the meantime?'

'That sounds great. We could open this if you like?'

Rory hands me the champagne, and I nod my head in approval before hurrying into the kitchen and taking out four champagne flutes.

The sound of a cork popping out of a bottle usually signals the beginning of a celebration, but Drew doesn't look like he's in the party mood as he makes an appearance downstairs, looking noticeably pale, although I suspect that is all to do with Alice being here rather than anything he consumed earlier today.

Faking food poisoning. He must think I was born yesterday.

'Cheers!' I say after I have handed everybody a glass and we all toast, although some of us more enthusiastically than others.

I ask Drew to kindly seat our guests at the dinner table while I dish up the food, and he reluctantly does as I say, leading the couple out of the kitchen as Rory chatters away about what a wonderful home we have here, while Alice follows silently behind.

'This looks wonderful,' Rory says once I've started delivering the food to the table and, as I suspected, the combination of cooked meats and salad that I've prepared looks like it's going to be a winner.

'Help yourselves,' I say as I signal to my guests that they are to tuck in, and they both begin adding food to their plates, while Drew sits listlessly opposite Rory and stares mournfully at his glass of champagne.

I find it amusing that my husband could have thought that he could come here, to this tiny village, and reignite his relationship with Alice without considering the possibility that I might actually befriend her myself and invite them over for dinner. But that's just my husband all over. He never thinks of others. Only himself. And look at the mess it has gotten him into now.

Perhaps unsurprisingly it's me and Rory who do most of the

heavy lifting in the conversation as we eat, while Drew and Alice mostly pick at the food on their plates and sip their drinks while being careful not to get caught looking at one another too much. We chat about life in Manchester and all that entailed, as well as about how Scotland is so close now and how it provides the perfect opportunity for quick weekend getaways.

'We should all go over the border for a couples' weekend!' I say, as if the idea has just come to me randomly and isn't something I'm just saying to make Drew and Alice squirm even more.

'That sounds like a fantastic idea!' Rory tells me, and he raises his glass to me before going back to his meal. I haven't failed to notice that he isn't eating particularly quickly, nor very much at all.

'Is everything okay with your food?' I ask him after watching him for a little while longer.

'Oh, yes, it's lovely, thank you. I've just not really had much of an appetite recently, I'm afraid.'

I can't help but glance at Drew then because I know he told me Rory had been to see him, and I wonder if this has something to do with it. My husband is also looking at the food on Rory's plate and has obviously noted how he isn't eating like a grown man should be.

'Are you feeling okay?' I ask Rory. 'If not, Drew could have a look at you.'

'Oh no, there's no need for that. Let the good doctor enjoy his time off.'

'He doesn't mind, do you, Drew?'

I put my husband on the spot, watching as he has to do the polite thing and say that he would be happy to have a look at Rory, if he would like that.

'How about we finish up our meals and then us girls will give you boys a moment together?' I suggest breezily, and I really should be nominated for some kind of acting award based on my performance here this evening. I'm doing everything in my power to make the two cheats at the table as uncomfortable as possible, yet, to them, I must just look like a woman who is overly keen to make a good impression.

Once the food is finished with, I clear away three empty plates, and one rather full one belonging to Rory, before I ask Alice into the kitchen with me, leaving the men in the dining room. When there, I tell Alice all about how wonderful it is to have made a new friend here before chatting excitedly about how we'll have to take a shopping trip together sometime soon in Carlisle and, of course, start planning that weekend for the four of us in Scotland. And the whole time, that bitch just smiles, sips her champagne and pretends like she is my friend right back, despite knowing exactly what she has already done to me before we even met. Maybe it's her who deserves the acting award. Then again, there's another big contender in the dining room right now in Drew.

Who's going to win?

Who's playing the best game here?

I can't wait to find out.

SIXTEEN

DREW

As bad as this awful dinner party is, it does at least tell me one thing that I'm grateful about. My wife clearly doesn't have the slightest idea that I've been unfaithful to her with Alice. If she did then there's no way she'd have this woman in her home and behave so friendly towards her.

At least that's something then. One positive to come out of this charade. I guess I have been as good at covering my tracks as I thought I had, and Alice has clearly done the same with Rory or he wouldn't be here either. Our respective partners think we are the perfect companions, so much so that they think we should all go to Scotland together and have a weekend away. While that is my idea of hell, it proves that they are as stupid as each other. If only they knew what Alice and I had done behind their backs, then they would stop quaffing champagne and cracking jokes. But more fool them.

Besides knowing that my secret is still safe, this dinner party has taught me something else, which is that there's definitely something wrong with Rory. Seeing how little food he ate during the meal, when it was clearly delicious and deserved consumption, is another sign that all is not well in his body. I wasn't the only one to notice it either. Fern did too, so much so that she insisted I do a quick check-up of the 'patient' after our main courses. Now I'm reluctantly going through the motions with Rory, prodding his stomach, asking him about his bowel movements again, and basically making it look like I care. For his part, he looks just as awkward about this as I am, and tells me not to worry about it before thanking me for not mentioning to Alice that I had come to see him the other day.

'Of course, mate. Doctor–patient confidentiality. I wouldn't dream of saying a word,' I reassure him before making a quick check on his pupils.

'Thanks, mate. There's no point worrying her. I'm sure it's nothing. I bet the blood test comes back clean.'

The blood test that went down my sink?

'Yeah, I'm sure it will, mate.'

I conclude my check-up of him by telling him he looks okay before reminding him again to come and see me if anything changes, and he promises me that he will. But it's clear to me that he is a lot more worried about his potential condition than he is letting on, and I think he should be because he wouldn't have accepted the offer of an extra check-up if he felt fine.

Despite everything, I can't help but feel a little sorry for him in that moment, so I try and cheer him up by suggesting we go and grab a beer in the kitchen.

'Sounds good to me, mate,' he says, slapping me on the back like I'm a long-lost friend who has just come back into his life after many years away.

While I am keen for another drink, part of my reason for wanting to get into the kitchen quickly is to check up on the two women already in there. I find Fern and Alice chatting as they prepare dessert.

'How's it going in here, girls?' I ask them, feeling like I've gradually warmed into the part I have to play tonight, and am doing a better job of pretending everything is okay now. Or maybe I'm just starting to feel drunk. I did drink rather a lot of champagne with dinner.

'We're great. Dessert is almost ready,' Fern tells me, before Rory asks where the bathroom is because he could do with going before the next course is served.

'It's just upstairs, second door on the right,' I tell him, but Fern offers to show him, I think because she's worried he'll accidentally stumble into the wrong room and come across all the boxes that we still haven't gotten around to unpacking yet. That's my wife. Always keeping up appearances.

As she leads Rory upstairs, I seize my chance to speak privately with Alice. Emboldened by the alcohol in my system, I put my hands around her waist and ease her towards me slightly.

'What the hell are you doing?' she cries under her breath, trying to push me away.

But I refuse to let go, keeping her close, if only to try and remind her of how we always used to be.

'You look so good tonight,' I tell her, whispering in her ear. 'Good enough to eat.'

'Drew, stop it. They could walk in at any moment.'

'I don't care. Maybe it's for the best. At least it would bring an end to this sham.'

'Drew, please. Stop it.'

'Why? I know you like it.'

I kiss Alice's neck then, and while she eventually pushes me away, it takes her a second or two to do it, confirming to me that she does indeed like it and that I'm closer to winning her back than I thought.

'I've got an idea,' I say to her, keeping my voice low as I hear the floorboards creaking above our heads, telling me that Fern and Rory are still upstairs and out of earshot. 'You should meet me at my surgery one night when my receptionist has left. We could be alone together there. You know, all doctors have a bed in their rooms for examining patients. I could give you an examination. And, of course, you'd be entitled to patient confidentiality. Nobody would ever know. What happens in that room stays in that room.'

I move closer to Alice again and have another go at kissing her neck, and she takes even longer to stop me this time. It's working. I'm getting her back. But she still puts up a little resistance, if only to keep me working for it.

'I'm not sure that would be a good idea,' she says, but that's as good as a yes to me, and my smile lets her know I'm already counting on it happening. But then she says something that dampens the mood somewhat.

'What's the deal with Rory? Is he okay?'

'Rory?'

'Yeah, you just had a look at him, didn't you? Is he all right, or is there something wrong?'

'I don't know. It's hard to tell. There's only so much I can do for him in my dining room.'

'He barely touched his meal. I've noticed he's not been eating as much at home either. I think there might be an issue.'

'Would it be a problem if there was?'

'What's that supposed to mean?'

'Come on, Alice, this is me that you're talking to. You don't have to pretend. I know he doesn't make you happy. You've told me as much before.'

'That doesn't mean I want him to be ill. He's a good man.'

'Yeah, but he's not as good as me, is he?'

I tug gently on Alice's hair then, and she lets out a soft moan before composing herself again.

'Did you really come here for me?' she asks me, warming up to all the attention she is now receiving, attention that I'm sure her husband doesn't give her in quite the same way.

'You bet,' I reply as I gaze down at her lips and see her nervously nibble her bottom one. She's falling under my spell again, just like she did in the early days. The fun days. But who says the fun has to stop now?

'You know we are meant to be together,' I tell her, growing in confidence with every passing second. 'Rory is a nice guy, but you don't want that, do you? You want a guy who knows how to treat you. A guy like me.'

Another tug on the hair. Another soft moan. Alice is putty in my hands now.

'And besides, if Rory is ill, it would be a shame, but you wouldn't choose a sick man over me, would you?' I go on, being slightly cruel but making sure I plant the idea in Alice's head that there is no point backing the wrong horse in this race.

'So, you do think he's ill?'

'He came to see me the other day,' I confess. 'And between you and me, yes, I do think there is something wrong.'

'Have you told him?'

'No, it's not for me to say. I'll have to refer him, and someone else can give him the bad news if there is any.'

'Have you referred him?'

'No, but I will.'

'You promise?'

'Yeah.'

And then it happens. My lips touch Alice's and every hair on my body stands on end.

The sound of the toilet flushing above our heads causes us to break apart, and I move over to the other side of the kitchen before Fern and Rory return, ensuring they won't suspect a thing has happened while they were away.

Fern quickly picks up where she left off with the dessert, while I get Rory that beer I promised him from the fridge. Then we all return to the dining room where we enjoy more food, or at least three of us do, because Rory declines his portion.

Poor guy. But there always has to be losers in life, and as long as I'm in the winner's circle then I can't complain.

'Cheers,' I say, taking my first opportunity to raise a toast this evening. 'Thanks for coming around, guys. This has been fun.'

And then I make eye contact with Alice as we all clink glasses because I want her to know what I am hinting at.

The fun has only just begun.

SEVENTEEN

FERN

I think that dinner party was a success. Both my guests left my home with smiles on their faces. I had no complaints about the food, drink or overall hospitality that I put on, so I'm feeling pretty good as I lock the front door and prepare to go up to bed. It seems I'm not the only one feeling good though, because Drew is currently dancing around the living room to a song on the TV, a glass of wine held aloft above his head, and I've lost count of how many he's had this evening.

'Somebody's feeling better,' I say as I turn the music down a little. 'What happened to you being ill?'

'I felt much better once I got out of bed. I think the food helped.'

'And the wine, I'd guess.'

Drew laughs before finishing his glass and dropping down onto the sofa.

'That was fun,' he says, looking like he actually means it, which sets a few alarm bells ringing in my head, because it was supposed to be anything but fun for him.

'Really? You had a good time?'

'Yeah, they're a nice couple, aren't they?'

Okay, something definitely happened between him and Alice, and I'm guessing it was while Rory and I were out of the way upstairs. She must have been more receptive to him than she was that night down at the beach, otherwise he wouldn't be this buoyant now.

I'm sure if my husband was more sober he would be doing a better job at keeping a lid on his emotions, because even if something has happened with Alice, he'd still rather not have to get through any more hours of the four of us being together. With that in mind, I decide to bring him back down to earth with a bump by reminding him about the potential of a Scotland trip.

'I think it's a good idea. What do you think?' I ask him as I tidy up the room around where he lies.

'I don't know, maybe. There's no rush to organise it, is there?'

'No, but I imagine we'll be spending a lot of time with them both now, so we might as well make some more fun plans.'

I've done it. I've successfully quenched Drew's good mood by talking about future couples' dates for us, and now he looks a little grumpier again.

'So, what were you and Alice chatting about while we were upstairs?'

'What?'

'When I went to show Rory where the bathroom was. What were you guys talking about?'

'Oh, erm. Not much.'

'It must have been something. Unless there was an awkward silence?'

'No, it wasn't.'

'Then what did you talk about?'

'Erm, the weather.'

'The weather?'

'Yeah.'

'Wow, how exciting!'

Drew doesn't like it when I get sarcastic, but there's not much he can do about it in this instance.

'So, what did you two have to say about the weather?' I go on, teasing him more.

'Not much. Just how it was nice today.'

'Oh my God, it sounds like I missed the most exciting conversation in the world!'

More sarcasm. Drew looks uneasy. But I'm enjoying pretending he and Alice together are a boring combination, and I'm only just getting started. It's time to see how much he really likes her.

'I have to say, Rory does seem to be a lot more fun than Alice is.'

'What do you mean?'

'Oh, don't get me wrong, she is lovely. But she's a bit...'

'What?'

He really wants to know what I think of her.

'I don't know. Plain? Is that the right word?'

'Plain?'

I can see that he's hurt that I would call his mistress such a boring, average word. But if he doesn't like it then I'm only going to make it worse.

'Yeah, I mean, she's not the most charismatic person, is she? Rory is funny and has a bit of energy about him, but she's just kind of, meh.'

'Meh?'

'I don't know. Maybe I'm being harsh. I mean she is good-looking, but I just presumed she'd have a bit more about her.'

It feels good to be mean about Alice in front of Drew. I wish I could be harsher, but that would risk giving myself away.

'That's not very nice.'

'I'm just saying.'

'How would you like it if she said those things about you?'

'Calm down, why are you getting so defensive?'

'I'm not!'

'Yes, you are. You're defending her. Do you disagree with me?'

'I don't know.'

'I mean, you're the one who just told me that you had a chat about the weather, so that's hardly the most compelling argument against what I've said, is it?'

'Whatever, it doesn't matter,' Drew grumbles, and he clearly wants to drop it. But I'm enjoying myself too much to stop now.

'What's the matter? Does somebody have a little crush on our new friend? Is that it?'

'What? No!'

Drew looks horrified at the suggestion, or rather he's horrified that I've just come extremely close to stumbling upon his little secret.

'I mean, I'd understand it if you found her attractive. She is pretty.'

'No, I don't!'

'Are you being honest?'

'Yes!'

He's so pathetic. He can't even admit something as simple as that. He'd rather deny something that is blatantly obvious just to keep up with his other lies.

'Okay, calm down, I'm only teasing you,' I say, giggling to myself. But I stop giggling once I've left the room and am by myself again. I am troubled by the fact that Drew seemed in a good mood before I just started winding him up. I'm going to have to keep an even closer eye on him now, I suspect. If the affair is going to be back on again, I need to know about it immediately because, unlike last time, I am going to do something about it.

I finish up tidying in the kitchen before heading upstairs to bed, and Drew isn't far behind me. I actually hear him whistling in the bathroom in between brushing his teeth, and it's further evidence that he's in a good mood. It would be easy for me to regret leaving the pair of them alone together earlier in the night because it might have just brought them closer again, but there's no benefit to me trying to keep them apart. They'll do whatever they are going to do in the end, so I just have to let them get on with it and see how much of a hole they want to dig for themselves.

Drew slides into bed beside me, and the whistling stops, but that doesn't mean he's ready for sleep. That's because his hands start wandering beneath the duvet, moving across my body and letting me know that he is up for a little fun before we turn out the lights and call it a day.

All I can think is that with Alice on his mind, not to mention a load of booze in his body, he's feeling frisky, but I'm not sure how I'm supposed to make love to him when I know he'll be thinking of another woman the whole time. Then again, it won't be the first time I've had to do it. That's because despite his extra-marital activity, Drew has partly managed to make the effort to keep up in our bedroom, probably aware that losing all interest in sex with me would only raise a red flag and make me start to suspect him. So, like a good sport he is, he's always made sure to try and keep two women happy and not just one.

'Are you in the mood?' he asks me as he starts to kiss my neck, and he's so used to getting his way with women that it probably hasn't crossed his mind that I might say no to him. But I do, although not in such a blunt way. Instead, I just say something that I know will dampen the mood, because taking about ill health is hardly an aphrodisiac.

'I'm worried about Rory. You'll give him good care if he comes to see you, right?'

'What?'

'As his doctor, you'll look after him?'

'Of course I will, just like I would any other patient.'

'Good.'

Drew has stopped kissing and touching me now, and I take the opportunity to turn off the light and roll over.

'Sleep well, hubby,' I say through gritted teeth.

He doesn't say anything back.

EIGHTEEN

DREW

I've been staring at the blinking cursor on my computer screen for the last ten minutes as I consider whether or not to continue typing the letter I have already started. It's a referral letter for Rory, and I've been compelled to start working on it after he came by to visit me today and told me that he was now experiencing worsening pain in his abdomen.

He asked me during that consult if I had received the blood test results yet, so I had to fob him off with an excuse about how there was a backlog and things weren't running quite as quickly as they usually did. He believed me, just like any patient believes what their doctor tells them, and he left it at that. In fact, his next question was about whether I enjoyed myself at the dinner party, although he might have just been changing the subject to keep himself from worrying about his deteriorating health.

It's clear that the guy needs to be looked at by a specialist, not just a general practitioner like myself, and despite what I did with the blood test, I can't play games anymore. I'm going to get him whatever help he needs, which is obviously the right thing to do. But I'm aware that my sudden willingness to help out a man whom I considered to be my love rival has only occurred once I realised that I was actually beating him after all. The closeness of the moment I shared with Alice on Saturday night at the dinner party gave me the belief that we were getting back on track, so now I'm less worried about Rory and him getting in the way of us.

So, with all that said, why haven't I finished the letter? It probably has something to do with the fact that I'm also waiting for Alice to message me back.

I've sent her an invite to join me in my surgery after opening hours this evening, when everybody else has gone home and we have the building to ourselves. Like I told her on Saturday, we could have some fun in my room, nobody would have to know about it, and I've not wasted any time letting her know that I'm still keen for us to arrange a date.

I've not received a reply yet, so I'll add a few more words to this letter in the meantime.

When my phone does beep, I snatch it up off the desk and check it. When I read the message, I fist pump the air before jiggling my legs a little in my chair for good measure. That's because Alice has agreed to come and meet me here tonight.

Now all I need to do is make up an excuse for Fern.

I could say that I'm working late, but that carries with it the risk that she might come down here to surprise me with some cooked dinner or just to say hi. Better to say that I've left work completely and gone somewhere else. Maybe I could say I've gone for a drink with Julie. Call it a bit of team bonding or something like that. Fern won't think that's suspicious, nor will she get jealous, because she knows Julie is way older than we are. That's it. That's the excuse I will use. And that's how I'll keep my wife in the dark while I bring my mistress back into the light.

After sending messages to both Alice and Fern, I return to finish Rory's letter. But there's one more hiccup. The server seems to be down again. Even when I'm trying to help Rory, the fates seem to be conspiring against him.

I end up having to leave the letter for the time being while I deal with the last couple of patients for the day, and by the time Julie pokes her head around the door and tells me she is leaving, I've forgotten all about it. That's because with her now going home, the coast is clear for Alice to come inside.

I wave off my friendly receptionist before messaging Alice to tell her to meet me at the front door. There's just enough time then to apply a little of the aftershave that I keep in my desk drawer, and slick back my hair with my comb that I always keep handy too, before I leave my surgery with a spring in my step and go to welcome in my guest.

'Someone smells nice,' she says when she sees me, but that's all she can get out before I pull her inside, close the door and put my lips to hers.

Technically, it's not the first kiss we have shared since I moved up here, because we did have that very minor smooch in my kitchen the other night. But this is the first kiss where we don't have to worry about anybody catching us, and as our lips mesh together, it's a wonderful feeling to know that nobody is going to come between us until we've done what we both desperately need to do.

It takes us a little while, but we eventually make it into my room, where I close the door before unbuttoning my shirt and tossing it to the floor, before getting to work on the buttons on Alice's blouse. She tells me one more time how we shouldn't be doing this, but that's about the sum total of her resistance before she joins me in a half-naked state, nowhere near as shy as most of the patients who stand awkwardly in this room whenever I ask them to remove any items of clothing so that I can examine them more thoroughly.

The rest of our clothes fall off easily before we make our way over to the examination table, the place where I usually ask my patients to lie down if I ever need to do a little poking and prodding around as part of my investigations. But the table is being used for another reason entirely now and is going to double as a makeshift bed. As Alice and I pick up where we once left off back in Manchester, all my worries wash away. I forget about Fern and how I'm breaking the vows I made to her on our wedding day. I forget about Rory and how I've not acted professionally while he's been under my care. And I forget about how I had to leave behind everything I knew just to be here to have a chance at experiencing this pleasure again. But that's the power Alice has over me. She makes me forget everything and just exist in the moment, and that is a very powerful thing, far more powerful than any drug I have ever tried in my lifetime. Even though I'm supposed to be a proponent of good health, I have to confess to trying a few.

Once we've both done what we needed to do to feel whole again, we lie back on the bed with our bodies intertwined, our chests rising and falling as we wait for our normal breathing patterns to resume. It feels like neither of us wants to speak and break the perfect silence that exists between us, because to do so might break the spell we are both currently under. Eventually, Alice has something to say as she lays her head on my bare chest and allows me to stroke her luscious hair.

'What's wrong with us?' she asks, sounding genuinely concerned.

'What do you mean?'

'I mean why can't we just be happy with what we've got? Why do we feel the need to take these risks?'

They're good questions, but for me they're also easily answered.

'Because we know that life is for living, not regretting.'

'Fern and Rory are such good people though.'

'Maybe so, but that doesn't mean we're bad.'

'Doesn't it?'

'No, because it's not that clear cut. It's murky and grey, like everything else in life.'

'I suppose. But don't you feel bad for making Fern move up here under false pretences?'

'No, I don't,' I say confidently. 'Because what she doesn't know can't hurt her.'

NINETEEN

FERN

Do I buy Drew's text about him going for a drink with his receptionist tonight? Maybe if I was still under the illusion that he was a faithful man. But that illusion was shattered a long time ago, so now I think everything he tells me is a lie, including this. That's why I have left my house and ventured into the village to prove myself right. I'm on the hunt for my husband and, more specifically, I'm on the hunt to catch him with *her*.

But where to find them? I ruled out the beach because, while it's dark out, they would still be risking being seen together in public, so they surely wouldn't be so stupid as to get together there. I also figured that they wouldn't be so foolish as to try and book themselves into a hotel room, because there aren't many of them here, and it wouldn't be a good look for the village doctor to be seen taking out a room with a woman who was not his wife.

That's one thing I bet they'll miss now they have left the city behind. There were plenty of places they could take their sordid little selves in Manchester but not so many here.

So where else could they be?

The possibility that they could be meeting in his surgery has crossed my mind, which is why I'm generally walking in the direction of Drew's workplace. But, just in case, and by some miracle, he is telling the truth, I plan on calling into the pub on the off chance that he is having a drink with Julie. After all, if he was, that's the only place in the village they could go to have it, so I walk through the door with the tiniest bit of hope in my heart that, for once, he might have been honest with me. *Surprise, surprise.* Drew is not here, nor is Julie. But a familiar face is. Rory is sitting by the bar, and when he sees me walk in he gives me a wave. I really don't have time to hang around though, so I just give him a quick wave back before walking out again and carrying on towards the doctors.

When I get there, it's no shock to see that the building is all closed up because it is six o'clock and, unlike in Manchester, places here close at 5 p.m. prompt. But just because it looks like the place is empty doesn't mean it is, so I start to walk around the building, peeping in a few of the windows while careful to stay out of view of anybody who might be on the other side of the glass.

Most of the windows are shut, but I find an open one, and while the blinds are drawn across it on the inside, there is a slight gap every time the breeze blows. As I peer in, I see a bare leg, and while I can't see much else from this angle, I don't need to know who the leg belongs to. It's Alice's, because I can hear her voice. She's talking to somebody and asking them what happens next.

'Let's just take things slowly,' comes the response from a male voice I know all too well.

It's Drew. He's in there with her. And as the blind flutters slightly in the wind, I get more of a view into the room. And then I see the pair of them naked and in each other's arms, looking happy and contented, having no doubt just been very intimate with each other.

That's all the confirmation I need to know that the affair is back on again now, so I should just leave and go back home. Yet I find myself unable to leave the window, stuck there momentarily as I feel my heart breaking all over again. Despite suspecting this might happen again if I agreed to move here, I always held out a tiny bit of hope that my husband would change his ways and choose me in the end. But without this, I'd have always been wondering. We could have stayed in Manchester, though there was nothing stopping him from starting another affair there, and in a big city it would have been far easier to conceal. At least I can keep a better eye on him here, but it doesn't matter anyway. He's still a cheat, and now there is no doubt what I have to do.

I detect a whiff of aftershave as I stand by the window, and it's a scent I recognise. It's the aftershave I bought Drew for Christmas, although he hasn't worn it much since, presumably because he can't be bothered to make much of an effort to smell nice around me anymore. But he's obviously applied a little bit of it today, and that extra effort he has made with Alice is yet another small dagger to my heart, a heart that is now full of wounds, wounds that may never properly heal.

I hear a few whispers followed by some giggling, and then the unmistakable sound of deep, passionate kissing, and I know I should move on. But I'm being more of a spy than a voyeur, so I stay a little longer.

I finally tear myself away from the window just before I hear the sounds of lovemaking drifting out of it, and as I hurry away I almost feel like I'm the one with a shameful secret to hide. It feels wrong to have been snooping, but I'm not the one in the wrong here. I refuse to feel bad about what I've just done. I've done what I needed to do, and it's not my fault they have ended up being so predictable.

I think about going into the pub on my way home and telling Rory what I have just seen, but there'll be time for delivering the bad news to him later. I'll let him enjoy his drink for now, because it might be the last drink he enjoys for a while. It's another selfless act of mine in a life that is full of them, but armed with what I know now, I am ready to make a change and start being selfish.

What I want to do to Drew and Alice is something I've been dreaming about for a while, but almost never thought I would have the courage to go through with. It's a dangerous plot, but it's one that I have gone over and over in my head for a long time to the point that I feel like it might be bulletproof. Now I'm going to have to put it into motion, although it's not my fault it's going to happen.

It's theirs.

I'm so lost in my thoughts that I almost step out in front of a car as I'm crossing the high street, and I have to apologise to the driver who must think I'm an idiot for not paying attention to where I'm going. Maybe I'm an idiot in other ways too, and as I make it onto the road that runs along the beach, I look out across the water and feel lonelier than I ever have in my life. While my husband is cuddled up with Alice, I'm all by myself, but I don't mind the feeling because it's giving me the strength to forge on with what I need to do over the coming days.

My husband and his mistress have picked the wrong woman to mess with, but I'm sure it hasn't even occurred to them that I might be capable of what I'm about to do next. If it had then they would surely have ended their affair almost as quickly as it began, and there's no way Drew would have been stupid enough to follow Alice up here. But they don't have a clue, and that will be their downfall.

I arrive home and keep myself occupied with menial chores around the house until Drew walks through the front door ninety minutes later, whistling another tune and grinning from ear to ear.

'Good day?' I ask him as he walks over to give me a kiss with that same mouth he was kissing Alice with less than an hour ago.

My first thought is to recoil from the incoming kiss, but I fear that will give away knowing something is wrong, so I force myself to accept it, however much it will make me feel sick inside.

'The best,' he says triumphantly in response to my question. 'I'm so glad we moved here.'

I bet you are, I think as he plants his lips on me before swanning away to go and shower. *Enjoy it while you can, because it's going to be the last place you ever see.*

TWENTY

DREW

I slept like a baby last night, and not just because Alice wore me out in my surgery. It's because I'm completely at ease now with my decision to take the risk of moving to this village, as it's paid off spectacularly. I'm reunited with Alice, and life is worth living again. There might still be obstacles ahead, namely our respective partners finding out, but this isn't the time for worrying about things going wrong. This is the time for basking in the warm glow that comes from knowing my scheme to get Alice back has worked.

I'm in such a good mood that I decide to leave my car at home and walk to work this morning. It helps that the sun is shining again, though I doubt even a few raindrops would have dampened my mood as I left the house and strolled along the seafront.

Thoughts of Alice are the only thing filling my mind, and all I want to know is when will I see her again? I ask her that exact question via text as I make my commute. I know I'll have to wait a little while to get a response, because Alice always sleeps in late, but I can't imagine it will be a disappointing answer. She had as much fun as I did yesterday, so I'm sure she'll be eager to do it again as soon as possible.

But, rather annoyingly, I end up seeing Alice's husband before I see her, because Rory is on the high street as I walk along it. When he sees me, he makes a point of coming over to say hello.

'Hi, mate. How's things?'

'Yeah, good thanks. You?'

'Not bad. Still not feeling one hundred per cent but got to get on with things, right?'

'I guess.'

'Any idea when I might hear about my referral?'

Damn it. I still haven't sent that letter yet.

'Oh, it should be anytime now. I'll chase it up today.'

'No worries, mate. What about the blood test?'

'Oh, I'm sorry. There was a mix-up there. Some delays. Everything's slower since the pandemic, I'm afraid. I'll check for an update when I get to work.'

'Don't worry. I'm sure you've done everything you can. Well, I better get to work myself. I just popped out for some milk. Have a good one!'

Rory gives me a slap on the back before heading on his way, and I watch him go, unsure what I feel most guilty about. Playing games with his health or playing games with his wife. Probably best not to dwell on either too much though.

The rest of my walk to work is uninterrupted, and after saying good morning to Julie, I sink into my desk chair and prepare for another day of deciphering the hypochondriacs from the genuinely ill. Before I give the green light for the first patient to come through my door, I consult with the calendar on my desk and try to figure out if there might be a date coming up when I could whisk Alice away for a romantic night in a hotel somewhere. I guess it would have to be in Carlisle as that's the biggest place nearest to here, although any decent size hotel will do as long as it's far enough away. I didn't have this problem in Manchester. Back there, I could take my pick of places to book us a room, but I'm hardly going to try my luck with Betty's B&B on the high street. I bet she could spread gossip around this village quicker than I could say 'busybody'.

The idea of pretending to Fern that I have a medical conference to attend elsewhere comes to me mid-morning, and I figure that will be how I excuse myself from the village for a night. All I need to do then is find a way for Alice to get out of here too, but I'm sure she can help me throw around a few ideas when I see her next. And that next time will be very soon if the message I've just received is anything to go by.

Hey you. Yesterday was so much fun. I want to see you again. Meet me by the rocks at the beach at 8 p.m. I'll bring a blanket. I'm sure we can keep each other warm x

Alice wants to meet me at the beach tonight for round two? Brilliant. We've never done it on the sand before, probably because there's not many beaches in Manchester.

Tonight is the night.

I'll be there. Cant wait x

The rest of my day goes by spending more time daydreaming about Alice's body on the beach rather than listening to what some of the folks in the village have wrong with them, but I do take the opportunity to actually send Rory's referral letter today. That tells me I'm not as bad a person as I was beginning to fear I might be. Then again, I could hardly risk completely neglecting my duty of care to him.

Not after what I've done before, and I'm not just thinking about the blood test.

Despite being a distinguished doctor to date, there are two

incidents in my professional past that threatened to derail my carefully cultivated career path. The first occurred when I was still in the process of trying to qualify as a doctor, and sitting one of the many exams a person must pass if they wish to gain their licence to practice medicine. Despite never having cheated on any exam previous to that, from primary school tests to GCSEs and everything in between, I was suddenly feeling a little overwhelmed about the size of the task in front of me. So much to study. So much to learn. And so much pressure, knowing that one bad result could derail everything I was trying to achieve.

After several nights of bad sleep due to a combination of exam stress and too much enjoyment of the more fun aspects of student life, I realised I stood very little chance of passing an upcoming exam. But I also knew I wasn't the only one and, after overhearing a fellow student talking to somebody I didn't know in the library one night, I realised there was a way to guarantee better results in the test. The mystery person was selling access to the upcoming exam paper and, for a fee, a student could read it, find out what was coming and prepare accordingly.

I wrestled with the decision for a few days, delaying the inevitable because I wanted to believe that I could pass the exam just through sheer hard work and grit alone. But it became obvious to me that I was struggling after I failed a couple of mock exams I had made myself take and, so, with just two days to go until the big day, I procured a copy of the test paper, exchanging cash, and several of my morals in the process, for a sneak peek.

I hated myself for it, but it did the trick. I passed the exam and, after that scare, I vowed never to get myself into a position like that again. I worked harder, partied less, slept better and managed to pass every other exam with flying colours. But the memory of the one time I let myself down lingered with me long after graduation and into my fledgling career as a junior doctor, and it lingered so much that one night, several years after I did the deed, and after a couple of bottles of red wine, I confessed my sin to my wife.

Fern was shocked when I told her what I had done as a student, not least because she felt I was clever enough to have passed and didn't need to have done such a thing. Like me, she was worried what consequences my cheating could have on my medical licence. Could everything be discredited on the back of that one mistake? We both liked to think not, but we both also had a feeling it wasn't as simple as that. So best not to risk it and keep it quiet forever.

Some might say it would have been better if my secret had got out and I had lost my right to practise as a doctor, as there was another mistake looming on the horizon, a far more destructive one, and this time it wasn't just me it would affect.

The second incident was eight years ago when I took pity on one particular patient who came to see me, to tell me they were struggling to sleep after the recent loss of their partner. As well as suggesting counselling, I prescribed the man with sleeping pills, giving him the recommended dose to at least allow him to get some rest in between processing his grief. Unfortunately, that wasn't enough, and he returned to tell me that before asking for more.

I was initially inclined to disagree with him and advise that I couldn't give more, which legally was correct. But as he told me more about his struggles, I had started to wonder if I might be able to help him after all. Maybe it was because he was a similar age to me, perhaps it was because he mentioned he supported the same football team as me, or it could have just been because I felt so sorry for him and couldn't imagine what he was going through, but I ended up writing him an extra prescription, one that increased the dosage of sleeping pills, even though it was obvious at that stage that they weren't working and he needed professional help. It was also obvious that he was abusing alcohol because I could smell it on him when he was in my surgery. That was why I made sure to give him the warning to not combine the pills with the booze because to do so carried risks.

In hindsight, I should never have given extra sleeping pills to a man I suspected of being an alcoholic, but I did, and when I learnt of that man's overdose a few days later, I was devastated. I also did something else that I would end up regretting, which was confide in Fern what I had done. I shouldn't have done that, but I did, and after I'd told her everything about how I chose to give strong tablets to someone who would potentially mix them with a lethal amount of alcohol, she wanted to know what would happen next.

Would I be investigated? Be struck off the medical register? Be sued by the deceased's family? I told her that I would be okay, so long as nobody else knew what had happened.

So that became our little secret as well.

Those two secrets have been between us ever since, and while both incidents are a long time ago now, they are still things that hang over me and make me reluctant to officially leave my wife. The fear that she might make a call to the medical board or the family members who lost a loved one is very real, and why wouldn't she if she found out I was leaving her for another woman? Even leaving her without mentioning Alice makes me nervous, because she could still feel so aggrieved after I leave her as a middle-aged divorcée. I feel like I'm trapped in our marriage. I might be worrying about nothing, but considering that Fern has knowledge that could negatively affect my career, I consider it best to keep her feeling favourable towards me. There's no way she'd do anything to jeopardise me while we were still happily married, or at least from her point of view anyway, but if we were separated then all bets could be off. Of course, I regret ever confessing my sins to my wife, but I did so when we were much closer, and I genuinely thought I would be happy with Fern forever. How was I to know I was going to meet someone else and fall hopelessly in love at a later date? But since that has happened, my confessions have been like an albatross around my neck.

Along with that to contend with, there's also my knowledge that my wife does not react well to any hint that I might be getting close to another woman, and that knowledge was gained through harsh experience. It was a few years ago now, but it's still something that is seared onto my memory, much like a scar around which the skin never truly healed after taking damage. I'm referring to a time when I was messaging an old friend from my medical school days, Lisa, and someone who I admit I was intimately involved with in my younger years.

The fling Lisa and I enjoyed in our twenties came to nothing because we were both young, with our whole careers and lives ahead of us, and if I'm honest it was mostly about the sex. But when Lisa started messaging me years later, when I was married to Fern, I didn't think anything of replying to her and enjoying the conversation. After all, the messages weren't inappropriate in any way, just two old friends getting back in touch and learning how the other one was doing in life. Unfortunately, Fern didn't see it that way. A message from Lisa flashed up on my screen one night, which Fern noticed and, despite me insisting it was innocent, she went berserk, almost throwing my phone against the wall, calling me a cheat and even threatening to leave me.

It was a serious overreaction, or at least it was the way I saw it, but at the time I was simply focused on calming my wife down and proving to her that I was not being unfaithful. I managed to do that by showing her that there was nothing in any of the messages that could be construed as me sleeping with, or trying to sleep with, another woman, and nothing more was said about the matter. But that incident did play on my mind a little bit, although I was too embarrassed to mention it to any close family or friends at the time, because they all know Fern and I didn't want them to make judgements against her or me. The only person I did mention the incident to was my friend Greg, after one of our weekly tennis matches a few years ago. He'd been cheekily trying to get me to engage in a little harmless flirting with a woman while we were enjoying a post-match beer one night, but I shot that idea straight down by telling him that my wife would kill me if she thought I was up to no good, using the story of what had happened with Lisa's message to illustrate my point.

Greg agreed with me that it did seem like a major overreaction on Fern's part, but we put it down to the complexities of the opposite sex and how men will never truly understand women before moving on to talk about football. It has occurred to me that perhaps Fern reacted the way she did to Lisa's messages as a deterrent, to show me that it wasn't going to end well if I ever did push my luck and get close to another woman. I figured she wasn't crazy, just clever. Although I guess it didn't completely put me off the idea of seeing another woman outside of my marriage. When Alice came along. I didn't give a second thought to what had happened in the past.

Of course, I was well aware that my affair with Alice was like a child playing with fire, and still am now. But it certainly could be damaging if the truth gets out and Fern decides she wants to get some revenge on me, either personally or professionally.

All I can do is hope it doesn't ever come to that.

TWENTY-ONE

FERN

It's nice to have options when it comes to revenge. Thinking about how I could make my husband pay for restarting his affair with Alice gives me plenty of ideas, some much more sinister than others. Surely Drew must know that he is taking a huge risk by seeing another woman behind my back, and I can only assume it is a risk he has carefully calculated and learnt to live with anyway.

But what does he think might happen if I was to catch him?

If I had to guess, I'd say the worst that he thinks might happen is that I'll tell somebody about what he did with one of his patients four years ago, the one who was abusing alcohol and struggling to sleep, so Drew had prescribed more sleeping pills instead of referring him for help. The night Drew came home from work looking dishevelled and disturbed is one I'll never forget, because it was the night he let me in on a secret that could be potentially ruinous for him.

The fact he confided in me showed how worried he was, as well as how much he loved and trusted me back then. Although it makes me feel sad now because, after what has happened since, I know he doesn't feel that way about me anymore. We're way past the point of him telling me another deep and dark secret again, and if he does have any more, it's probably Alice who hears them these days rather than me. But he did tell me that sorry tale about his patient, as well as his history of cheating on important exams, and I'm sure he regrets confiding in me, because he knows I could use those things against him if I ever felt the need to get back at him.

I wonder if that's why he hasn't just left me yet. Maybe he feels he never can. It still hasn't stopped him from getting his fun elsewhere though. But is that it? Does he think the worst thing that might happen to him if I find out he cheated involves me trying to ruin his career? If so, that's hilarious, because he's severely underestimated me. Sure, he's right to be worried about me finding out about Alice. But it's not his career he should be worried about.

It's far more than that.

The only time I ever gave him an insight into how dangerous things could get for him if he cheated on me was when I found out he was messaging an old friend from his student days. I'll admit I might have overreacted at the time, particularly because there was nothing incriminating in any of the messages, but I couldn't help it. I was paranoid and afraid, and even though that came to nothing, I thought it would serve as a good warning as to what might happen if he ever was stupid enough to betray me.

I guess my warning wasn't forceful enough.

I'd worried in the days following whether or not I'd been too forceful, too overdramatic. But I'd also worried that I hadn't gone as far as I could have done. I should have thrown his phone against the wall instead of just threatening to, and that would have made a far more dramatic statement. You live and learn, as they say, and I certainly learnt from that experience, enough to know that when it came to something like that, instantaneous eruptions of anger weren't necessarily the best way of doing things. That's why I reacted very differently the next time I had cause for concern regarding the man I married.

'I've found us a movie to watch,' I call to Drew from my position on the sofa while he's out in the hallway. 'And don't worry, it's not another rom-com.'

I'm just about to press play on the remote control when he tells me he has other plans for his evening.

'Oh, sorry, love, but I was going to go for another jog. You don't mind, do you?'

'Another one?'

'Well, yeah, one isn't enough unfortunately.'

He laughs at his joke, and I make sure to laugh too, if only to make it seem like I'm believing every word he says.

'Wow, somebody really has got the fitness bug, haven't they?'

'I'm trying.'

'Fine, I guess I'll spend the night by myself then.'

'You won't be complaining when you have a toned Adonis of a husband in a few months' time.'

'Why's that? Am I marrying someone else?'

Drew rolls his eyes at my lame joke before telling me he'll try not to be too long, but if he gets the urge or the energy to extend his exercise then he might just keep going. I'm sure he's got the urge for something all right, but I obviously don't say that to him as I bid him farewell and listen to him leave the house.

While I know he is lying to me again about going for a run, using that as a smokescreen for going to meet Alice instead, I don't have to go chasing after him now. Unlike last time when I followed him down to the beach, I can take a little longer before I go in pursuit of him, and that's because this time, I know exactly where he is going.

I'm so calm that I actually manage to watch the first five minutes of the movie I found before I eventually spring into action, putting on my shoes and coat but making sure to leave my phone where it is on the arm of the sofa. I don't need to take that with me, nor should I if I am planning on playing it safe, which I most definitely am.

It's a cool and breezy night as I make my way along the street before cutting off the road and heading onto the sand in the direction of the rocks. I can't see my husband at the moment, but I know he'll be ahead of me somewhere, because there's nowhere else in the world that he would rather be right now with what he has in mind.

I glance back over my shoulder as I walk across the beach, seeing my house in the distance, but looking more specifically at Audrey's house and the other neighbours' properties nearby. But they're a safe distance away from where I'm headed, and with the darkness factored in too, there's no way anybody in those houses is going to be able to see what is happening down here on the beach tonight.

With no worries about witnesses on land, I then turn my attention to the water. I look to see if there are any boats out there that could have people on them, people who might have a good view of the sand and what is about to happen on it very shortly. The last thing I need is a fisherman to ruin all of my best-laid plans, but there are no vessels out there. All is quiet and calm, which is always the best way for things to be right before all hell breaks loose and things can never be the same again.

It must have rained a little earlier because the sand is sticking slightly to the bottom of my boots, but it's not difficult enough to make me want to stop and go back. I suspect it's also not wet enough to dissuade Drew from wanting to roll around on this sand with Alice shortly, or at least that's what he thinks is going to be happening.

I can see him now, up there ahead of me. He's made it to the rocks and has taken a seat on them. He's a few minutes early, so he's got time to look out across the same quiet body of water I just did, and I bet he's feeling very zen right now as he enjoys a peaceful moment before his woman arrives.

Oh, his woman is going to arrive all right. It just won't be the woman he was expecting.

It's at this point that I realise I am at the threshold, and it's my last chance to change my mind before I cross it. Once I do, I can never go back. This is it, the final moment where I can choose for my life to go one way or the other. It's already too late for Drew, he has made his choice tonight and is committed to it. But it's different for me. I could change my plans. I could go back and sit on the sofa and watch that film and have a very easy few weeks ahead of me. Or I could keep going, do what I am planning to do to Drew and perhaps alter my destiny forever.

In the end, it's a very easy choice.

I keep going, walking right up to the rocks and making just enough noise on my arrival to attract Drew's attention, so that he turns and looks towards me.

He's expecting Alice.

But he's got me.

'Fern, what are you doing?' he cries, jumping up off the rock as if it was suddenly burning his backside.

'Doesn't look like you're doing much running,' I say with a wry smile. 'What's the matter? Not as fit as you thought you were? Or just not as clever?'

'What are you talking about?'

'I think you know exactly what I'm talking about. I'm talking about the real reason you left the house tonight, because it certainly wasn't to go for a run, was it?'

Drew glances around nervously as if to check that Alice

isn't going to turn up here and cause a problem for him, and maybe he doesn't realise that it's already too late for that.

'Who are you looking for? Are you waiting for somebody?'

'No, of course not.'

'Are you sure? This looks like a pretty good meeting point. The rocks on the beach at 8 p.m. And look at that, it's eight o'clock on the nose.'

I tap my watch, and I think it's then that it slowly starts to dawn on Drew that I haven't just stumbled upon him acciden-tally. I knew he was going to be here at a specific time.

'How?' he asks me when he realises I've set this meeting up.

'How what? How did I find out you were having an affair with Alice? Or how did I get her to message you to tell you to meet her here?'

Drew keeps looking around the beach as if Alice is still going to be joining us, but I shake my head at him.

'Forget about her. She isn't coming.'

'Fern, I really don't know what you think is going on here, but I just came out for a run tonight. I was tired, so I sat down for a minute on these rocks, but I was going to go again in a minute.'

'Can you just stop lying for one second and admit that you've been caught out?'

'I don't know what you mean?'

'So, you're not going to admit to your affair then? You're not going to give me the decency of coming clean now that I've caught you out? You'd rather just keep lying even if you know it's pointless?'

Bless him, he really has no idea how to answer my ques-tions, so I make it easier for him, and offer him a few questions of his own.

'Ask me when I found out about you and Alice,' I tell him, and while he doesn't want to do that, I keep insisting until he does.

'When?'

'In Manchester.'

'What?'

I can see that answer shocks him. Maybe he was thinking he only got rumbled a couple of days ago at worst, but, no, he actually got rumbled months ago, and I'm enjoying seeing him realise that.

'That's right. I found out about you back there. So, the next obvious question is why did I move here with you after what you did to me?'

'Why?'

'Because I was giving you a chance.'

'A chance? What do you mean?'

'A chance to live.'

'What the hell are you talking about?'

'All you had to do is stay away from Alice. Not restart the affair. Show me that you had changed. If you'd done that then we wouldn't be here now. But you couldn't help yourself, so here we are.'

'I really don't know what you're talking about.'

'I saw you with her in your surgery. You told me you were having a drink with Julie. But you were with Alice. Naked. Kissing. Laughing. Who were you laughing at? Me and Rory?'

Drew must know he can't deny it if I saw him, yet he still tries anyway.

'It's not what you think. I can explain.'

'Let me take a guess. You accidentally messaged me and told me a lie, then Alice accidentally came to your surgery before both your clothes accidentally fell off and you ended up on the bed. Is that it?'

I'm being ridiculous, but only because Drew is too.

'Fern, please, let me just explain.'

'No, let me explain. Let me tell you what's going to happen

next. I'm going to walk off this beach and go home and get on with my life without you.'

'Fern, please. Divorcing me isn't the answer.'

'Who said anything about divorce?'

That confuses him, just as I thought it might. It also makes me laugh because this is it. The moment I've been waiting for.

The moment my husband pays for what he has done.

TWENTY-TWO

FERN

I lean against the back of the front door after I've closed it and take several deep breaths.

Come on, Fern. Keep it together. Stay calm. It's no good losing it now.

Once I've composed myself, I carry on with what I need to do, and my first job is to put my clothes in the washing machine.

I strip off in the kitchen before bundling my clothes into the machine and activating a spin cycle. Then I watch the soapy water running over my garments for a moment through the circular window before picking up my boots and taking them to the sink. There, I scrub them clean until every grain of sand is removed, so nobody would ever know that these boots have been down at the beach tonight or any other night for that matter.

Leaving my boots to dry on the draining board, I go upstairs to take a shower, and the hot water on my skin revitalises me, just as I was once again at the point of potentially losing control of my emotions.

It's over with now. You've done what you had to do. Now you just need to stay calm, and everything will be okay.

That shower ends up being the longest one of my life, thanks to all the washing, crying and laughing that I do during it. I'm all over the place in here, but by the time I turn the tap off and reach for my towel, I have my game face back on, and that's okay because as long as I keep these little meltdowns in private then nobody will ever suspect a thing.

I dry off thoroughly before adding my towel to the basket for the next lot of washing. Then I put on my pyjamas and go downstairs to make a cup of tea, making an effort to try and get back into my pre-bedtime routine, because that's important.

Everything I do from here on out is important.

With a hot tea in one hand and a digestive biscuit in the other, I curl up in front of the TV for half an hour and try to decompress before bed. It's not easy, but I find some distraction in watching the national news, until I eventually have to change the channel when a report comes on about a murder trial currently underway in London.

For some reason tonight, hearing about a person in court on suspicion of a serious crime is not something I fancy learning more about.

I get restless after a little while, so go to check on the washing machine and, with its cycle complete, I can take out my clothes so they can start to dry. I also make sure to put my boots back under the stairs before cleaning the kitchen, so it doesn't look as if a worried woman has been in it, scrubbing everything she had on this evening.

I make it into bed not long after ten o'clock, but the space beside me on the mattress is unavoidable. Drew would usually be here now, lying next to me, and we'd normally have a brief chat before the light went out, and his snoring started. But not tonight. He's not here, nor will he ever lie beside me again.

Sleep won't be easy to achieve, but I have to try, so I wrap myself in my duvet and force myself to think about something relaxing. People say to try counting sheep when you want to drift off, but somehow, I don't think that's going to cut it for me. Instead, I try counting all the times that I know Drew has lied to me in the past. That's surely a far greater number than any amount of sheep I could ever dream of.

I don't drift off for several hours, but I do feel justified in my actions the more I think about all of Drew's failures in our marriage, to the point where any guilt I might be feeling about what I've done fades away, as easily as the darkness outside my window once the sun begins to crest on the horizon.

I must have fallen asleep at some point around dawn, because when I wake up it's almost nine o'clock, and I've slept in a little later than I was planning on doing. The first thing I reach for upon waking is my phone, on which I type out a short message to my husband, one that might seem a bit banal, but will prove to be very important as I look to project my innocence in the eyes of the police officers who will be looking into me over the coming days.

Hi, love. Sorry I didn't see you before you left for work. I've only just woken up. Thanks for sleeping in the spare bedroom last night. I'm feeling much better now. I hope you have a good day. Can't wait to see you tonight. Love you x

With that vital task complete, my next job is to get up, get dressed and get to the church hall in time for the weekly coffee morning. Showing my face there is another important step in making it seem like, as far as I'm concerned, everything is still normal in my life.

No dramas. No cause for concern. *No reason to call the police.*

A quick cup of coffee perks me up before I leave the house, and I make it to the hall right on time for the start of the meeting. The chairs have already been set out, the cups have been filled with tea, and the regular attendees are in the building, chattering away between themselves and treating this like it's just another normal Wednesday in the village, which it is, for now, at least.

'Good morning, Agatha,' I say, remembering the name of one of the women I spoke to here at the last meeting, and she looks pleased to see me. Maybe she isn't going to be as pessimistic about everything as she was last week. But that optimism lasts all of ten seconds before she starts moaning to me about how the tap in her bathroom has been leaking for the past few days and driving her mad at night with the *drip, drip, drip* sound.

Listening to her is akin to listening to a leaking tap all night, but I force myself to do it because I can't behave in any way out of the ordinary. I sat and put up with this woman's stories last week so I must do the same this week. I also must talk to the other people that I'm seated near, so that each and every one of them will be able to recall seeing me here should the police reach out to them to corroborate any of my story. If they do, I need all these women to say that everything seemed normal with me, and I didn't look like a woman who knew something was seriously wrong with her husband at that time.

Alice is here, as she should be in her role as organiser of this meeting, and I make sure to have a few words with her before it concludes. But when I get the chance to interact with her, I can't help but notice that she seems troubled by something.

'Is everything okay?' I ask her after detecting a bit of grumpiness.

'Yeah, it's fine. I've just lost my phone. Can't find it anywhere. Very annoying.'

'Oh, that's a shame. Can you remember the last place you had it?'

'Yeah, it was at home, but I can't find it. I've looked all over, but no sign of it.'

'I'm sure it'll turn up.'

'I hope so.'

'I'm always losing my phone. But I always get it back. Try not to worry about it. Just have another look when you get back. And, if worst comes to worst, you'll just have to treat yourself to a new one.'

'I'm not sure my husband will be happy about that,' she says, picking up a couple of used cups and putting them on a tray.

I'm just about to give her some help when my own phone rings, and I take it to answer the call quickly.

'Hi, is that Mrs Devlin?' the female voice at the other end of the line asks me.

'Yes, it is. Who is this?'

'My name is Julie, I work at the doctor's surgery with your husband, Drew.'

'Oh, hi Julie. Is everything okay?'

'Well, I hope so, but I'm not sure. You see, Drew didn't come to work this morning, and I was wondering if he was ill.'

'Drew's not at work?'

Alice hears me and stops what she is doing, but I'm happy for her to eavesdrop on this conversation, so I don't make any effort to move away from her.

'No, is he with you?'

'No, I thought he was there. I mean, when I woke up, he wasn't in the house, so I presumed he'd gone to work.'

'Oh, I see, but he's not here, I'm afraid. Do you know where else he might be?'

'No, I've got no idea. Have you tried calling him?'

'Yes, but his phone is off. I was hoping you might be able to help me.'

'I'll have to try him myself. This is very strange. Just give me one moment, and I'll call you back.'

I end the call and try Drew's phone.

'Is everything okay?' Alice asks me, but I just give her a

puzzled look before going through the motions of ringing my husband. But as I already knew would be the case, he doesn't answer, so I call Julie back to tell her I've had no luck reaching him either.

'I've checked his diary to see if he had any conferences or anything today, but there is nothing in there,' Julie tells me, sounding as confused as I'm pretending to be. 'Did he say anything before he left this morning about having somewhere else to be? It's just we have patients here waiting to see him, and I'm not sure what to tell them.'

'No, I didn't see him this morning. We slept in separate bedrooms last night. He was giving me some space as I was feeling unwell. He was gone by the time I woke up.'

'This is very strange.'

'Yes, it is.'

Alice is still standing next to me, and while she can only hear my side of the conversation, she's heard enough to know that something might be wrong with Drew, which means she isn't going anywhere until she finds out what it might be.

'I'll try and find him,' I tell Julie. 'Please can you call me if he turns up?'

'Yes, of course. I'm sure he's okay. Try not to worry.'

'I'll try.'

I hang up then and go to leave, but, as I thought she might, Alice stops me.

'What's happened? Is Drew okay?'

'I don't know. He seems to be missing.'

'Missing?'

'He didn't show up at work this morning.'

Alice looks very worried now, far more worried than a new friend should be.

'Where do you think he might be?' she asks me, but I just shrug and say I have no idea. Then I excuse myself because I have to go home and check if he's there, and I leave Alice standing beside the table of teacups, no doubt watching me go and no doubt wishing she hadn't lost her phone so she could try calling Drew and check if he's okay herself.

But she doesn't have her phone.

And based on what I know, she is not going to find it.

But the police might.

TWENTY-THREE

FERN

I've kept calm and carried on doing what would be expected of a wife whose husband's whereabouts seems to be unknown. After leaving the church hall, I went straight back home to 'check' the house for any sign of Drew. Having found none, I rang Julie again and asked if there was any news there.

'No, I'm sorry. He's still not here,' she had told me, and I feigned a little more concern before telling her I might have to go to the police.

'Oh, I'm sure it's not that serious,' she had said, trying to calm me down, but without any hint of where Drew could be, there wasn't much more she could say to dissuade me from making my next call.

I dial 999 and ask to speak to a police officer, and after giving my name and address, I'm allowed to get to the point.

'It's my husband,' I say hurriedly. 'He's missing.'

'When did you last see him?'

'Last night before I went to bed.'

'And what was he doing?'

'Going to bed as well. We slept in separate rooms.'

'Any particular reason for that?'

'What do you mean?'

'I'm just wondering if perhaps there was a disagreement.'

'No, nothing like that! I was just feeling unwell, so he thought I might get a better night's sleep if I had the bed to myself.'

'I see. When did you notice he was missing?'

'I didn't. It was only when I got a phone call from his workplace. The receptionist there told me he hadn't come in.'

'You didn't see him this morning?'

'No, I had a lie-in.'

'What time did you wake up?'

'Around nine.'

'And your husband was gone?'

'Yes.'

'Did you hear him leave?'

'No, I was asleep like I said.'

'So, he could have left the house last night?'

'I don't know. I don't think so. I thought he was going to bed.'

'But you never saw him get into bed?'

'No.'

'And he hasn't gone to work today?'

'No.'

'How does he get to work? Does he drive?'

'Usually, but he sometimes walks if the weather is nice. The car is still here, so I assumed he had walked today.'

'Okay, where does he work?'

'At the doctor's surgery in the village.'

'How long would it take him to walk there?'

'Oh, I don't know. Half an hour, maybe.'

'Would that be along a busy route or side streets?'

'It's a village. There's not really any busy route here.'

'Okay, I'm just trying to ascertain whether he might have been seen on his way to work this morning. Have you had a walk around? Asked anybody if they have seen him?'

'No, isn't that your job to do?'

'Well, yes, we can do that, and we certainly will if your husband has not made his presence known somewhere soon, but it's still very early, so we can't officially call him missing yet.'

'But he is missing! If he's not at work, where is he?'

'He could be in any number of places.'

'But his car is here, so he can't have gone far!'

'Okay, please try to stay calm.'

'Calm? I'm worried sick here!'

I feel like I'm doing a very convincing job of being the distressed wife who just wants to know that her husband is safe, and after a little panicking on my part, I'm told that a police officer will be sent to my address to speak with me further.

'In the meantime, have a look around the house and see if there's anything that might give a clue as to where your husband might have gone.'

'There's nothing here! I've looked!'

'What about his wallet? Is that there?'

'I can't see it.'

'Okay, just hold tight and somebody will be with you soon.'

The call ends, and while I'm sure the police officer I just spoke to feels like she has left me in limbo for a little while, I'm simply ticking off another item on my mental checklist of things to do today. Now that the police have been alerted to the fact my husband is not where he should be, I must prepare myself for some questions from them face to face. But that's okay, I knew this was going to happen, and it's all a part of what needs to occur before the inevitable happens.

I decide that it might be better for me to stay in character while I wait for the police to get here rather than chill out on the sofa with a drink and a biscuit, so I hurry around the house, opening drawers, rummaging through wardrobes and generally doing my best to make it appear like I have searched the house for any sign of where Drew might have gone.

I'm in the spare bedroom looking under the bed when I hear the car engine at the front of the house. When I peep out of one of the upstairs windows, I see the easily distinguishable colouring of the vehicle that has just parked.

The police are here.

'It's okay,' I tell myself as I head for the stairs. 'They won't be worried at this stage. But it's perfectly fine for me to be.'

I thank the officers for coming as quickly as they could before telling them I followed the other police officer's advice and searched the house but didn't find anything that might shed some light on this mystery. Then I have to go through the whole story again, answering all the questions I already answered on the phone, because I guess they weren't debriefed on the situation before they got here. Or maybe they were, and they are just asking me all of this again to see if I change one of my answers, a simple slip-up that could signal that I might have something to do with the disappearance after all. But I have spent so much time rehearsing the story in my head that I know it word for word, so I have no problem recalling everything I have already said and repeating it for the two officers sitting across from me.

'Has anything like this ever happened before?'

'As in him going missing? No.'

'He's never had an unexplained absence from work?'

'Not that I know of.'

'And there's never been a time when you didn't know where he was if you needed to contact him?'

'No, he's always where he should be. And he always answers his phone or texts me back if I am trying to reach him. Always.'

The police officers seem to be getting a good idea of why I am so worried now because I keep mentioning how strange it is for Drew to not have his phone on so I can reach him.

'How would you describe his state of mind over the last few days?'

'What?'

'Has anything happened that might have troubled your husband?'

'Like what?'

'It could be anything. Something at home. Something at work.'

'No, nothing. We were great, and he was enjoying his new job.'

'New job?'

'Yes, we've just moved here from Manchester. He's the new doctor in the village.'

'Did the move go smoothly?'

'Yes.'

'Has your husband indicated that he might have been missing Manchester?'

'No, it was his idea to move here.'

'And why was that?'

'He likes it up here. I do too. It's more peaceful.'

I am being very careful to make sure I keep referring to Drew in the present tense rather than the past. All it would take to mess this whole thing up would be talking about him as if he was no longer with us, because the police would surely pick up on that and start asking me much more difficult questions.

'He hasn't been stressed or anxious about anything?'

'No, why? Do you think he's in trouble?'

'No, not at all. We're just trying to build a better picture of him.'

'Well, as far as I know, Drew has been fine. I'd have known if something was on his mind because he tells me everything.'

It's an absurd lie but the police don't know any better. To them, we could have been the perfect couple who were so in love with each other, and this could just be a big misunderstanding. I'm happy for them to keep thinking that for as long as it takes.

'Okay, thank you for answering all of our questions. If you don't mind, we'll have a quick look around here, and then we'll go into the village and knock on a few doors, ask around and see if anybody has seen your husband. Somebody's bound to have, and I'm sure once we start looking, we'll find him pretty quickly.'

I get that these police officers have been trained in how to deal with a worried member of the public, and what they have just told me is supposed to put my mind at ease. I'm sure their training also told them that somebody isn't going to stop worrying just because of a few words, and it's only action and results that will make a difference in situations like this. Action like going to look for my husband and results like finding him.

I remain on the sofa while the police officers have a look around the house, but I'm confident there is no piece of incriminating evidence that they might discover that could lead them to the truth. They call me up to the spare bedroom after a few minutes and ask me if the bed looks like it had been slept in, because the duvet and sheet are tucked in, which suggests not, but I say I'm unsure.

'Maybe. I don't know. It's hard to tell. He could have made it again before he left this morning, I suppose.'

That's a vague enough answer to not help matters, which is just what I needed, and the police officers don't have any more questions for me, probably because they've realised I'm past the point of being much use to them now.

'Okay, we're going to go and have a walk around the village and see what we can find out about Drew's most recent movements,' I'm told.

'And what should I do?' I ask, awkwardly holding onto the side of the banister at the bottom of the stairs, and acting as if I need the support that it's offering me because I'd otherwise be too weak and worried to stand.

'Just sit tight, and we'll be in touch. But do give us a call if your husband comes home.'

'Of course. I will.'

The officers leave, and I let out a sigh of relief because it's another test passed. But that's merely the easy bit done with. The next time I'm in the presence of the police won't be so simple for me.

I won't just have to answer some questions then. Instead, I'll have to give the acting performance of my life. I'll have to weep and wail and beg whoever is listening to tell me none of this is true and that it's all just a bad dream. When they can't, I'm going to have to drop to my knees and let out the kind of cry that could send a shiver down the spine of anybody unfortunate enough to hear it. And after all of that, I'm going to have to act like I have no idea why somebody would want to hurt my husband so badly because he was just a wonderful man, and he definitely didn't deserve the horrible fate that has befallen him.

But first things first.

Time for a cup of tea and a biscuit.

TWENTY-FOUR

FERN

I made sure to savour the last few moments of quiet calmness in this village, aware that once the body was found on the beach then it would be a long time before peace was restored to this part of the world again.

For a part of the country that very few people seemed to be interested in, I knew that this would soon be somewhere that all sorts of people were suddenly fascinated by. Journalists, who would never have imagined something interesting could happen around here, would come scurrying in from the towns and cities, their pens poised for a quote, their cameras and recorders ready for a soundbite, all eager to get back to their editors with something juicy that would help give them a leg up in their careers.

Local police officers who have grown bored over the years, for having nothing to deal with but the occasional drunk driver and a bit of petty theft at the local supermarket, would suddenly find the passion for justice reawakened inside of them, and they would spend the next several days desperate to be the one person who could crack the case and be the hero.

And then there's all the people around the country, people

who never give a second thought to an English village just outside Scotland because why would they? But soon they will care. Soon they will be turning on their TVs, and tuning in their radios, and searching on their smartphones for the latest bit of news from here, a place that gives them just enough drama and intrigue to make them forget all about their mundane lives, wherever they live.

It's all going to change soon.

Everybody will be looking in this direction.

Everybody will be looking at me.

Some will feel sorry for me. Losing a husband is a horrible thing to have to go through. But others will suspect me. 'It's always the wife,' they'll say with a sly grin, as if they are actually basing that on some kind of evidence rather than just being deliberately controversial. Of course, those who suspect me will be a lot closer to the truth than those who don't, but that's not the point. The point is that whichever way I look at it, I'm going to be talked about.

I'll be profiled in the newspaper. My age listed beside my name, as if it matters how old I am. Depending on the quality of the journalism in question, there might even be a reference to my looks in a way that a man would never be subjected to. 'Pretty Partner Devastated by Husband's Murder' or something along those lines, as if what I look like is as important as what has happened to me.

I wonder what photo will be used. Do I get a choice in that? Can I give them one or will the journalists just take one of mine from social media, not even giving me the chance to pick how I'm portrayed? The journalists who are painting a picture of a devastated wife might choose a modest one, maybe of me in a buttoned-up blouse with very little make-up on. But those who have an agenda and suspect me will probably use one of the photos of me on holiday, in a bikini, a big smile on my face, as if

I'm just a fun-loving girl who doesn't stop for anything, not even the loss of her husband.

Some journalists will ask for permission to speak to me, while others will just stick a microphone in my face and hope that I talk. There may be financial offers to get my side of the story, but it wouldn't be a very good look for me if I was to accept them, so I will make sure to turn them all down firmly.

I'm going to have to deal with all of that on top of handling the police, but that's just what happens when a serious crime occurs and nobody knows who committed it. At least I feel like I'm ready for it all, and that's a good thing because, after I have just got out of the shower and started to dry my hair, I hear the first sign of things changing in the village.

It's the siren from the ambulance outside, and as I rush to the window I see it moving off the road and onto the beach, its wheels spinning over the sand and churning it up, the tyre tracks left in its wake likely to remain there until the tide comes in and washes them away.

I watch the ambulance as it gets closer and closer to the rocks, the same rocks where I stood last night with Drew as I confronted him with the truth. That only seems five minutes ago, but in reality sixteen hours have passed, and it's not taken quite as long as I thought it would for somebody to find what I left behind. At least I assume that's why the ambulance is here now. Maybe it's been called out for another reason. But what are the chances of there being two bodies out there on the same day?

I watch as the ambulance comes to a stop, and I see two figures get out of it before they disappear from view. They must be with the body now, checking for signs of life, administrating CPR, doing anything they can to revive it. I wonder how long it will take them to realise that it's already far too late?

Evidently, not long at all because then the police cars start arriving, and that's the point at which I decide to share my knowledge of what is happening down here at the beach with somebody else. I take out my second phone, the one I purchased as a burner so it couldn't be known about to any police officers in the near future, and make a call. When it's answered, I convey as much information as I need to in as few words as possible.

'They've found him.'

My simple statement is understood, so I can end the call almost as quickly as it began before I hurry to get dressed, so that I'm ready for when one of the police officers on the beach decides to come and pay me a visit.

I think about going outside to make it look like I'm curious as to what might be going on, and I bet a few of my neighbours are already standing on their doorsteps with a frown on their face and their arms folded, shocked and annoyed that something so serious could be happening right outside their homes. I'm sure Audrey is out there somewhere, and, knowing her, she's probably already baking something that she can give the emergency workers to eat in case they get peckish during their latest shift. But I mind my own business and keep my front door closed, preferring to act oblivious to what is going on just outside the limits of my property, and happy enough for somebody to come and tell me without me asking any questions first.

It takes a while but, eventually, there's a knock at the door and I know it's the police coming to tell me that Drew is dead. I wonder which poor man or woman has drawn the short straw and has to be the one to tell me that I'm now a widow. It must be somebody with experience in this kind of thing, but I suppose it could be somebody who is having to do it for the first time. If that's the case, then they're probably almost as nervous as I am as the door opens and the formalities begin.

'Mrs Devlin?'

'Yes.'

'I'm PC Monroe, and this is PC Knight. Could we come inside, please?'

'What's happened? Have you found my husband? I reported him missing earlier. Do you know where he is?'

'If we could come inside and then we can talk.'

'Oh my God, what is it? What's happened? Is he all right?'

I then look past them at all the vehicles on the beach and really ramp up my acting.

'Oh no, does all this have something to do with him? Is it my Drew? Is he hurt?'

'Please, can we come in?'

I step back and let the officers enter, and they invite me to take a seat on my sofa, as if I'm a guest in their home and not the other way around. Only when I'm seated do they hit me with it.

'I'm terribly sorry, Mrs Devlin, but we believe we have found your husband, and I'm afraid it's bad news. A body was found on the beach by a dogwalker a short time ago, and I'm afraid there was nothing anybody could do for him. We suspect it's Doctor Devlin due to the visual identification made by a couple of bystanders down at the beach, although, of course, we'd need you to formally identify the body. And we sincerely apologise for the fact that there were bystanders down at the beach, but I hope you can appreciate it is a very difficult place to contain.'

I deliberately say nothing, opting to just stare back at the police officer, who I guess has done this before because he's quite assured. Either that or he's got a natural talent for it, but that would be a very weird and rather unfortunate talent to have.

'Mrs Devlin, are you okay?'

I should probably say something now.

'Drew's dead?'

My question is barely audible.

'We believe so.'

'What happened?' I ask, raising the volume of my voice a little but still trying to sound somewhat meek and deflated, as if all the air has been drained from my body after being given such terrible news. I'm also staying stone-faced for the time being, but the waterworks are on their way, and when they start they will be worth the wait.

'It's too early to say, but the forensic teams are investigating, and we'll update you as soon as we have more information. But we do need you to identify the body, if you feel like you can.'

'I don't understand. You found him at the beach? What was he doing down there?'

'We don't know yet.'

'I don't understand. How did he die? Did he drown?'

'Again, we need to let the forensic teams carry out their work before we can give you all the facts. In the meantime, try not to speculate or do anything that might cause you any distress.'

'Distress? You've just told me that my husband is dead! How do you want me to be?'

Now it's time. The tears well up in my eyes, and I give it all I've got, letting them run down my cheeks as I wail and whimper, running through all the five stages of grief in almost as many seconds.

'No, this isn't happening!'

'How could this happen? Tell me! How?'

'No, tell me anything else but this. Please!'

'I can't believe he's gone! How am I going to cope without him?'

'He's really gone, isn't he?'

The officers do the best they can to console, which involves getting me tissues, putting an arm around me and even making me a cup of tea. Of course, I have to make out like none of it is working and that there's nothing they can possibly do to make this better, until the time comes for me to say that I want to see him.

'Of course,' Officer Knight says, and he helps me up off the sofa, one of his hands on my quivering arm as I make sure to keep shaking, so it looks like I really am in a state of shock. Then he helps me into a car, and as we drive away I see Audrey standing outside her house, watching me go.

She looks utterly helpless.

Thankfully, I'm not feeling the same way.

TWENTY-FIVE

FERN

The room where Drew's body is being held is cold and characterless, which is funny because it makes me think of my husband's heart and how it was the same in his final days. I'm led into the room by a very sorry looking man in a white coat, and as he begins the process of revealing the corpse on the gurney, I wonder what on earth possessed him to get into this line of work.

How bad could it be to think that this was the best job for you? Unless he's one of those morbid types who actually likes being around death on a daily basis. Well, rather him than me because, while I have to be around it now, I'm very much looking forward to getting this over with.

I take a deep breath and dry my eyes with a tissue before I give him the nod and, on my command, he pulls back the cover and shows me what is kept underneath it.

It's Drew, though never as I have seen him before.

His once rosy cheeks are now pale, the colour drained out of them long before I came in here to see him this last time. His eyes are closed, so it could just look like he was sleeping if I wanted to try and make this situation more bearable, but the specks of blood on his T-shirt and neck quickly remind me that there's no way this is going to be anything but torturous.

The droplets of blood shine brightly beneath the fluorescent lighting above our heads, but I do wish the power would go out, so I didn't have to see it all. At least I can only see some of it. There is a lot more blood around the back of the head, a part of the body that isn't visible to me and a part that I do not care to see even if it was offered. I know all that because that's where the telling blow was struck, the blow that ended my husband's life and put me on a path that ends here, with me in this room beside this man who is now about to ask me a question.

'I know this is very difficult, but is this man your husband?'

I stare at the body for a few more seconds before nodding my head and putting my hand to my mouth, so he knows I'm simply too shocked to speak. I make sure to cry as the body is covered up and I'm led back out of the room, and I keep crying all the way into a conversation with the next person to have a very tough job.

It's the detective in charge of figuring out who killed Drew.

Looking like a cross between a bad football manager and a dodgy department store mannequin, the man standing in front of me in a grey blazer, black trousers and a very cheap pair of shoes introduces himself to me as Detective Tomlin. He offers his condolences, before asking me to take a seat and wondering out loud if he could perhaps have somebody get me a drink.

'No, thank you,' I say, shaking my head and doing my best to stifle a few more sobs.

'Again, I'm terribly sorry for your loss,' he says before pausing and looking a little awkward. 'I just have a few things that I need to go over with you, if that's okay?'

I nod my head, my body language giving off the impression that I just want to get this over with quickly, so I can go home and start making funeral arrangements.

'Your husband died as the result of a trauma to the back of

the head,' Detective Tomlin tells me. 'We believe he was hit by an object and died instantly.'

I make sure to act appropriately stunned, even though I know that is exactly how he died.

'What I am going to do is find out exactly who delivered that blow and make sure they are brought to justice,' the eager detective goes on, possibly getting a little thrill from delivering a line that could be straight out of a TV crime series that couples binge-watch over a weekend.

'One of the things I need to ask you is if you know of anybody who might have wished your husband harm?'

'No,' I say, the wet tissue in my hand soaked in snot and tears.

'He had no enemies? No one who might have held a grudge against him for whatever reason?'

'No.'

'Did he have any arguments or disagreements in the days leading up to his death? Try and think, it doesn't have to be something big. It could be something as simple as him not stopping to let another car out or someone spilling their pint against him accidentally in the pub. Anything at all that might give me something to look into.'

'No, I can't think of anything.'

The tissue in my hand is gradually being ground down into a tight ball, and I should probably put it down but it's weirdly comforting. I need the distraction from this detective and his questions, even if it is only a minor one.

'What about you?'

'What about me?'

'Did you ever argue with your husband?'

'No.'

'Never? Wow, you must have been the first couple in the world not to fight.'

I realise I've been a little too eager to make out like we had no problems, so I quickly correct that by giving an answer that is a little more believable.

'I mean, of course we had minor disagreements like everyone does.'

'Like what?'

I'm already starting to hate this detective, but he shouldn't pose a problem to me as long as I keep calm and answer everything plainly.

'Just silly things. Quarrels over housework, whose turn it was to fill up the car with petrol. Nonsense really.'

'But never anything serious?'

'No, never.'

The detective nods but I'm not sure he believes me and that makes me uneasy. It is imperative that he does believe me and, as he makes me run through the story of the last time I saw him, I make extra effort to be as convincing as I can as I tell several lies.

'One thing is for sure,' he says with a shake of the head, 'your husband did not go to bed last night. He was dead long before dawn, which means he must have left the house some time after you had gone to sleep in the master bedroom. Can you think of any reason he might have chosen to go out?'

'Erm,' I say, pretending to be giving it some serious thought before it comes to me. 'He sometimes went for a jog.'

'A jog?'

'Yeah, he'd recently started doing it. He wanted to get fit. Lose some weight.'

'That might explain why he was found in clothes that could be used for exercise. Did he usually go jogging on the beach or elsewhere?'

'I don't know. I never went with him. I think he changed his route depending on his mood.'

'And you know that how?'

'He would tell me where he went when he got back.'

'What did you do while he was out jogging?'

'I usually watch TV but that night I guess I was asleep.'

'You guess?'

'I mean I was.'

The detective reclines in his chair, and the squeakiness of it is disturbingly loud in the otherwise silent room.

'How are you feeling?'

'Pardon'

'How are you feeling?'

'How do you think I feel? I've just lost my husband. I feel terrible.'

'No, I don't mean that. I mean your general health. No sore throat, cough, fever?'

'No, why?'

'It just says here that you were ill the night you last saw your husband, so I'm wondering what was wrong with you? It can't have been the flu because if it was then you've recovered remarkably quickly.'

He suspects me. He thinks I'm lying. I'm screwed.

'Erm, no it wasn't the flu. I had a headache.'

'Do you suffer from many headaches?'

'Sometimes.'

'And when you have these headaches, do you always make your husband sleep in the spare bedroom?'

'Sometimes.'

'Sometimes again. Okay.'

I don't like the way he's talking to me, but I think it's time to stop being defensive and be more assertive.

'My husband has been murdered. Why are you asking me these questions? You should be out there trying to find the person who did this.'

'Don't worry, my team is investigating and I'm confident they'll find the culprit quickly,' he replies. I don't miss the hint that is designed to make me worry, if I am indeed that culprit.

'Well, good. Because I want to know why they did this.'

'As do I.'

We stare at each other for a beat before I reach for another tissue to blow my nose, and it's just enough to break the tension that was threatening to build in the room.

'Okay, well, if I have any more questions for you then I know where to find you,' Detective Tomlin says. 'For now, on behalf of me and my colleagues, please accept our condolences at this difficult time.'

'Thank you,' I murmur before getting out of that room as quickly as I can.

As I suspected and feared, having to talk to a detective was a nerve-wracking experience, and an experience that I'm sure I'll have to repeat again. But, for now, I'm free to go home, where a counsellor will be waiting for me, so I'm not on my own until family members can arrive from Manchester.

I stare out the window of the vehicle that is taking me back to my house and, as we get closer to the village, I see the rows of parked cars and media vans on both sides of the streets. It seems even busier than the day of the fete, and I wonder what all the residents are making of this as their home is swamped with people trying to find out more about the murder on the beach.

For the first time since I've been here, I witness an actual traffic jam as a police van tries to turn around in a road that is not quite big enough for such a manoeuvre, but none of the motorists in the waiting vehicles honk their horns. They are all mindful of the fact that the police are only here to do a job and everybody needs to leave them to it until it's done.

The poor police liaison officer driving the van eventually realises that he needs to go the way he doesn't want to go before he can get to the way he does want to, and the traffic begins to move again, allowing me to get closer to home. But there's little respite there if the crowd of people outside my house is anything to go by. At first, I assume they are all journalists waiting to corner me as soon as I get out of the car, but then I see the bouquets of flowers and realise they are residents coming to pay their respects. Despite only recently identifying Drew's body, word must have already spread about the identity of the deceased. The dogwalker who discovered the body must have mentioned to somebody that it was the new doctor, and that piece of information has been spread like wildfire through this close-knit village.

Everybody turns to look when they see the car that I'm in approaching, and I wish there was another way I could get to my front door without having to face them all, but there isn't, so I take a deep breath before I'm escorted through the melee.

'I'm so sorry!' somebody shouts to my left.

'They'll catch whoever did this! I promise!' another person cries to my right.

A few more sentiments are shouted my way but mostly everybody is quiet as I pass them, unsure what to say or unable to say anything for fear of upsetting me even more. I see a few faces from the coffee morning, and I guess they have the perfect item for the agenda next week at a meeting that I'm pretty sure I won't be at. But there is one person from the meeting who isn't here and she's conspicuous by her absence.

Alice is nowhere to be seen and I wonder why.

I guess it's because she's too upset to face the world.

Unlike me, she has lost a man she cared about.

But there'll be plenty of time for catching up with her soon enough.

TWENTY-SIX

FERN

Flowers. I feel like I'm drowning in a sea of them. White lilacs or roses seem to be the go-to options for people looking to buy a gift for someone in need and, apparently, white is the unofficial colour of mourning, so I guess that makes sense. My house is now filled with bouquets that have been left by either loved ones or strangers, all combined in their desire to show support for me during this difficult time. Of course, I appreciate all the gestures, if not the amount of petals that are littering the carpet in the living room, but as anyone who delivers a bunch of flowers under difficult circumstances will know, they don't really make much of a difference. They don't change the bad thing that has happened or make everything suddenly okay again. They just add a brief bit of colour to brighten up the gloominess before they wilt and die and act as a further reminder that everything else in life tends to end up going the same way too.

I'm not technically in mourning, despite what everyone else thinks; I'm not feeling as bad as I could be as I watch another bunch of lilies get put into a vase, before being displayed on one of the few surfaces that still has room left on it to spare. The 'florist' in question is my mother, Kath, and she has been here for almost twenty-four hours now, arriving yesterday with my father, Tony, with sorrowful looks on their faces and their arms open wide to take in their beleaguered daughter.

I was actually able to cry quite easily when I saw them, not because I've got even better at this acting thing, but because I could see the genuine pain on both my parents' faces. It broke my heart to think that they believed I was going through hell. I could see that each of them would gladly do anything they could, if there was a chance that they might be able to take what had happened to me and transfer it into themselves, and even though they had no idea I was actually perfectly fine, it still made me upset to see.

They've both been busy since they got here, Mum organising the flowers and sympathy cards while making more cups of tea than I thought humanly possible, while Dad has been trying to cheer me up with tales of the good times, either from when I was a little kid and did something silly, or when Drew and I got married, highlighting something funny that happened on the wedding day. Some people might awkwardly skirt around the subject in a situation like this, but Dad isn't like that. He isn't afraid to mention Drew's name and risk upsetting me, not if there's a chance he can make me smile while thinking about him instead, and he is good at that. So good in fact that at one point, he makes me remember a time with Drew that was so good, I actually get genuinely upset over what I have lost.

It all looks like a natural part of the grieving process to them but, for me, it's a blunt reminder that despite what I planned and executed, I have still lost something. I lost all the good times that came before the bad. The joy before Drew brought the sorrow. There's no getting them back now, no chance for Drew to redeem himself, win me over again, renew our vows or anything like that. It's just finished. Forever.

One thing I am even more grateful for, even more so than

what my parents are doing for me, is the fact that I haven't had to face Drew's parents yet. They both live overseas and, while they're on their way over here now, they haven't made it yet, which I'm relieved about because I know the pain on their faces is going to be far worse than that on my mum's and dad's. It sucks that I've contributed to the grief they now have, and they could only understand why if they knew what I had been through and what it was like to be with a man who walked all over me for so long. But they can't know about any of that yet so, as of now, they are reflecting on the loss of their beloved son, cherished husband, popular friend and esteemed doctor in that order, despite the fact that some of those titles didn't apply to him by the time he died.

It's not just family members who have come to visit though. People in the village have called by, braving the horde of journalists in front of the beach to knock on my front door and deliver their condolences in person. Audrey has been here, and she was armed with baked goods, obviously. Agatha came, possibly enjoying the fact that she could be as miserable as she always is, and nobody would bat an eyelid in a situation like this. The owners of the butchers have been round to hand over a very large and very calorific tray of meats because, as they put it, 'Sausages can't help at a time like this. But they can't make things any worse either.'

Dad is currently in the kitchen cooking a few of those sausages now, and the smell is making my mouth water a little. But before I get to tuck into a tasty sandwich, there is another visitor to deal with and, after my mum has opened the door, I hear exactly who it is.

It's Rory. He's offering his deepest sympathies.

But all I want to know is if he has brought his wife with him.

I walk into the hallway to get a better view and, when I do, I see that Alice is indeed standing beside her husband. She is wearing a black blouse, as if she is already having a dress rehearsal for the funeral, although I'm not sure exactly when that will be. The police still have work to do with Drew's body before it can be laid to rest.

'I'm so sorry,' Rory says when he spots me lurking behind my mother in the hallway. 'If there's anything we can do. Anything at all.'

I force myself to step a little closer to them, and Rory really does look like he means what he has just said. Unsurprisingly, Alice hasn't said anything yet, and I wonder if she will even try to, but then she clears her throat and offers her condolences as well.

'Thank you,' I tell them, joining my mother who puts a reassuring hand on my shoulder as I tell her who these people are. 'These are new friends we made in the village. We had a dinner party shortly before Drew...'

I purposely let my voice trail off then, leaving my sentence unfinished because it should be hard for me to say the words.

'Drew was a great guy,' Rory says. 'We feel very fortunate to have known him, even if it was just for a short time.'

'Yeah,' a very sombre Alice adds, not that she needs to tell me how glad she was that she met my husband. She looks tired and her eyes are slightly puffy, suggesting she was crying before she came here. But I imagine she was doing that in private, out of sight of her partner, just like the affair she conducted for so long.

They both look like they are ready to make a move then, leaving me and my family in peace, that is until I suggest to them that they come inside for a drink.

'Oh no, we wouldn't want to impose,' Rory says, but I insist, making sure to take pleasure in how uneasy Alice is about the thought of having to come into this house again.

'I'll put the kettle on,' Mum says for the twelfth time today before she scurries into the kitchen, while Rory and Alice awkwardly follow me into the living room, where we all take a seat in front of the flowers.

'I still can't believe this has happened,' Rory says, shaking his head. 'Why would anybody want to hurt Drew? He was a great guy.'

I shake my head too, before mentioning that all I can hope for now is that the police find the guilty party.

'Do they have any leads at all?'

'Not that I know of.'

'I'm sure they'll catch them. They have to.'

'Yeah.'

There's an awkward silence then before it gets broken by the sound of sobbing. But it's not me crying this time.

It's Alice.

She does her best to stifle it, but I guess it's hard for her to do that because, unlike mine, her tears are very real and, as Rory gets her a tissue, I watch the weeping woman and wonder if she could possibly have loved Drew more than I did on our wedding day. Maybe, or maybe it was just all about sex between them. Either way, we've both lost him. But that doesn't mean we both have to be losers.

There's a bit of commotion outside my window and I ask Rory if he could peek between the closed curtains and find out what's going on, because if I was to look for myself then I'd just be photographed by all the camera phones out there.

He does as I ask and, after making a check, he tells me that police cars are parking up outside my house.

'I'm not sure what's going on,' he says before telling me that the police are heading up the driveway.

'Maybe they have some news,' Alice says optimistically as she dries her tears.

I'm guessing they have, otherwise why would they be here? But what do they know? Have they figured out who the killer is? Have they figured out what has really happened here?

'I'll get it,' Dad calls out as he goes to answer the door, and while I should go with him, I remain seated on the sofa, too anxious to stand up.

This could be it. The police might have seen through my lies. And now they're coming to arrest me in front of my parents and the woman I hate.

I hear low voices in the hallway before the sound of footsteps approaching, and it sounds like Dad has let several people into the house.

How many police officers are out there?

I get my answer when they start to file into the room and, after counting at least four, I take a deep breath and figure I better start trying to do a good job of acting shocked when they put the handcuffs on me.

But I'm not the one they are here for. Instead, they turn their attentions to the sofa opposite me.

'Alice Richardson, we are arresting you on suspicion of murder. You do not have to say anything, but it may harm your defence if you do not mention when questioned something that you later rely on in court. Anything you do say may be given in evidence.'

'Wait. What?' the suspect utters.

Alice looks as confused as everybody else in the room as she is lifted to her feet and her hands are pulled behind her back. The flash of metallic that I see is the handcuffs going on before she is marched to the door. But it's not going to be that easy for them to just take her.

'What the hell are you doing? That's my wife!' Rory cries, trying to stop them, but they obviously don't like that and warn him to let them do their jobs or they will have to arrest him for obstructing an officer.

'I don't understand,' Dad says as the smell of burning sausages wafts in from the kitchen.

Mum adds her confusion to the mix then by asking me what

is happening, but I just stare in disbelief as Alice is led away. I'm then told by another officer that I will be updated on the developments shortly and, as Rory demands answers immediately, I notice the tissue lying on the carpet where Alice's feet just were. She must have dropped it just before she was arrested.

Arrested for the murder of my husband.

I wish I was alone right now so I could smile.

I'd smile because what has just happened is good news.

It means that everything is going to plan.

TWENTY-SEVEN

FERN

I'm back at the police station and eager for my update from Detective Tomlin. While I wait, I imagine Alice in custody and how she might be dealing with all the questions being directed at her. She might be upset that she is being accused or she might be defiantly protesting her innocence. One thing is for sure though. She won't be going anywhere until the police are satisfied that she did not kill Drew, and if I have done my job right, they never will be.

Another hour goes by before the detective comes to see me, fresh from speaking with Alice, and as he sits down opposite me, he thanks me for being patient at what is a very difficult time.

'What's happening?' I ask, cutting to the chase.

'Well, as you know, we arrested Alice Richardson on suspicion of murder. We have been questioning her, and we feel there is sufficient evidence to detain her while we carry out a search of her property.'

'What evidence?'

'We found a message on your husband's phone from Alice,

in which she told him to meet her on the beach the night of his death. The location she suggested is the same location where the body was found.'

So far, so good.

'Oh my God, you think she killed him? Why would she do that?'

'We don't know the full story yet, but this is a very strong lead, and when we were questioning Alice, we asked to see her mobile phone, so we could confirm the message came from her device. However, she was unable to provide it, telling us she lost her phone a few days ago.'

'That seems very convenient.'

'Possibly. That's why there are officers on their way to search her home now. I'm going to join them, but I just wanted to keep you abreast of the situation before I go.'

'Do you think you'll find it? The phone, I mean.'

'I don't know. In the meantime, Alice will be held here because we still have plenty more questions for her. But that phone is key, so if you don't mind, I'm going to accompany the team during the search.'

'Of course. Thank you.'

Detective Tomlin leaves, and I'm escorted out into the corridor where my parents have been waiting for me.

'What's happening?' Dad asks me when he sees me. 'Did she do it?'

'They don't know yet. They're going to search her house.'

'I thought she was a friend!' Mum cries, so innocent and naïve, and I love her for it.

'I just want to go home,' I say. 'Drew's parents will be here soon.'

We make our way through the corridors towards the exit, but, before we get there, I hear somebody arguing around a corner. I recognise the voice as belonging to Rory, and perhaps unsurprisingly, for a man who has just seen his wife be arrested for murder, he is very angry.

'Somebody needs to tell me what the hell is going on!'

I know I should probably just leave, but I can't resist taking a look, so I walk towards the noise.

'What do you mean you want to search our house?' Rory cries. 'No, I don't give you permission to do that! I want to speak to my wife! This is ridiculous!'

I see Rory then, surrounded by policemen. If he's not careful, he might end up joining his wife in custody. That's because he's still ranting, and despite being repeatedly told to calm down, he isn't doing so.

I'm hoping the police officers will have a little sympathy for him, because I'm sure they would be just as frustrated if their own partners had been arrested for a serious crime and they weren't getting any answers. It's surely not helping that Rory knows his home is very shortly about to be turned upside down by some of those same officers searching the property, and even though he's saying he doesn't want that, they have a warrant, so there's not much he can do about it.

'Come on, let's go, love,' my mum says, wanting to get me away from the chaotic scene, probably because she thinks it's only going to add to the stress of the situation. But I keep watching just long enough to see Rory eventually concede and allow the officers to do what they need to do. He pathetically slumps down into a chair and buries his head in his hands, as everybody around looks relieved that they won't yet have to make another arrest.

As the officers disperse and go back to whatever they were doing before the noise started, my parents head for the door, and they think that I'm right behind them. But I linger and keep my eyes on Rory long enough to see him raise his head from his hands and make eye contact with me.

And when he does, he gives me a sign that he is okay after all.

He winks at me.

If only I was feeling a little bit bolder, I would wink at him too.

TWENTY-EIGHT

FERN

The array of shopping bags in my hands are a good sign that I've had a productive trip into the centre of Manchester today. As I climb into the back of a taxi and head for home, I'm feeling good. There's nothing like a bit of retail therapy, and while I'm sure my husband will be nervously checking the bank statements shortly after my latest splurge, he knows I never go too crazy when I'm armed with his credit card.

Poor Drew. He's at work now dealing with another busy day of patients. He works so hard, and I sometimes feel bad for having a much easier, carefree life than he does. But he's also extremely passionate about what he does and lives to help others, so I know he'd rather be there, in his surgery, prescribing painkillers and asthma inhalers rather than out here shopping with me.

I manage to make it into the back of a taxi just as the first few drops of rain are beginning to fall from yet another charcoal-coloured sky that hangs over this city. That might be the motivation I need to start thinking about a holiday getaway, somewhere warm and sunny, and I make a mental note to do a bit of research when I get back, so that I have a few locations in mind when I suggest to Drew that we take a little trip in the coming weeks.

He deserves a holiday, and it's been a while since our last one. Maybe we'll go to Italy again. Or perhaps further afield. A return to the Caribbean where we enjoyed our honeymoon could be an option.

It's easier to deal with the grim weather outside as I fantasise about all sorts of exotic places while my taxi driver takes me home. As he turns onto my street, I look forward to walking through my front door and dropping my many bags at my feet, before relaxing a little in the lovely house I have put so much time and effort into. It's a really homely place, and I can't see us ever leaving it. We got it for a good price and spent any money we saved on renovating it, and while it's surely gone up in value, I can't foresee a reason that Drew or I would ever want to sell up and move somewhere else. We love it here, not just in our property but in this area too. It's not that far from where we were both born and raised, with family and friends on our doorstep, so it has everything we need for a happy, healthy life.

And then I see the man standing at the top of my driveway, a stranger here without a reason I could think of, but someone who very shortly will deliver the news to me that will end up changing my life in more ways than I could ever imagine. But of course, I didn't know that as I opened the taxi door to climb out of it and, after the driver has driven away, I realise the man outside my house is definitely here for me.

'Hi, Mrs Devlin?'

'Yes. That's right.'

I eye the stranger up and down, noting his reasonably formal appearance and smart haircut, trimmed beard and warm eyes, and feel confident that he most likely isn't some weird serial killer or stalker who has been lurking out here waiting for me with bad intentions. But he does seem to know my name, or at least my surname anyway, so what the hell is this all about?

'Who are you?'

'My name is Rory.'

'Are you a friend of my husband?'

'No. But I know who he is. He's the reason I'm here.'

'Has something happened to him?'

I'm suddenly filled with fear that while I've been spending my day frittering money and dreaming of holidays, Drew might have been involved in some kind of accident.

'He's fine. Don't worry. But I need to talk to you about him. Could I come inside?'

'Out here is fine,' I say, not yet willing to let this man into my house without fully understanding who he is and why he's here.

'What is this about?'

Rory takes a deep breath before telling me.

'Your husband and my wife are having an affair.'

'Excuse me?'

'My wife's name is Alice, and she has been sleeping with your husband, Drew.'

'What the hell are you talking about?'

This might actually be worse than if Drew had had an accident.

'I found messages on my wife's phone last week. She was texting another guy. It was obvious they were close, so I followed her one day and saw her meet him outside a hotel. Then they both went in together.'

Rory shows me a photo on his phone of Drew and his wife entering a hotel in the city centre. It's him, there's no doubt about it, but there has to be another explanation for this.

'You must be mistaken. My husband is not having an affair.'

'I know this must be a shock to you, and I completely understand how you're feeling because I didn't want to believe it either. But it's true.'

'They could have been doing anything in that hotel. They might be colleagues going for a meeting or something!'

I'm clutching at straws, but I suppose there is a slim chance Drew might work with that woman, even though he's never mentioned her, and he could have been attending a medical conference that day in the hotel.

'How do you explain this one?' Rory asks me, showing me another photo and, this time, there is no way I can try and excuse it. That's because it's an image of Drew and Alice kissing on the street just outside the hotel before parting. A brazen act, one that not only removes all doubt about the nature of their relationship, but demonstrates just how confident they were about not being caught.

I feel like I'm suddenly losing the feeling in my legs as the shopping bags slip out of my hand, and I have to take a seat on my garden wall. It's as if my chest has just been put in a vice and is being squeezed, or maybe it's just my heart. I've never experienced pain like this before and I didn't know it was possible to feel so bad.

'I'm so sorry to be the one to give you this news, but I felt like you had a right to know,' Rory tells me, showing genuine concern for my wellbeing, which would be sweet of him if I didn't have too much other stuff to try and process right now.

'I can't believe this,' I say, my voice laced with a mixture of despair and disgust as the pain in my chest refuses to ease while my mind wrestles with two main questions: how could Drew do this to me? How am I supposed to go on living now that I know about it?

Rory must have already dealt with all of this because he is more composed than I am and tries to console me, not that it does much good.

'How did you find me?' I ask him, aware that I'll have a

better chance of getting an answer to that question than the two I previously thought of.

'I followed your husband back to his workplace that day, after the hotel, and saw he worked as a doctor. I wanted to go inside and pretend like I had an appointment or something, just to confront him. But I couldn't pluck up the courage to do that, so I just sat outside. I ended up following him home, to here, but again I couldn't face him. So, I just left. I got his name from a quick search online of the doctors who worked at that surgery. His photo is on their website.'

Thinking about not only what Drew has done with that woman, but that he has been followed by her husband, and still has no idea he has been rumbled, is all more craziness to add to this shocking situation.

'I don't know what to do,' Rory admits as he takes a seat on the wall beside me. 'I presume you had no idea anything was going on?'

'No, of course not!'

'I'm sorry, I didn't mean it like that. I've just been racking my brains for any signs of noticing this problem sooner, you know? But I thought we were okay. We rarely argued. We were happy together, or at least I thought we were.'

That sounds exactly like my marriage with Drew, so it's obvious we've both been completely blindsided by this.

'I don't know what to do either,' I admit, my voice shaking with emotion.

'I'm going to talk to Alice tonight. Tell her what I know.'

Rory seems a lot bolder than me, but then he has had longer to process this than I have. The thought of having a similar conversation with Drew fills me with dread, because I know that once I've uttered the words 'I know', then his façade will crumble, and I have no idea what he will do next. Will he get defensive and deny it? Will he spin me a story to try and excuse it? Or, and this is the thing I'm most afraid of, will he just admit that he has been having an affair, removing all possible doubt before telling me that he is leaving me for her?

'What are you going to do?' Rory asks me, and it seems as if he's seeking a little validation to confront his partner by hoping I'll be doing the same thing.

'I suppose I'll tell Drew that I know too.' But I'm already aware it's easier said than done. How am I supposed to confront the man I expected to be married to for the rest of my life and tell him that I know he's ruined it all for us? Because that is exactly what he has done. He has stolen our future while at the same time destroying what used to be a happy past.

It's four long hours after that conversation on my garden wall before Drew gets home from work, and I spent all that time doing my best not to be sick. But the nausea almost overwhelms me as he walks in and smiles at me, behaving as if everything is okay when, unfortunately for the both of us, it is not.

I should just come out with it. Say what I have to say. Get it over with.

'How's your day been?' Drew asks. 'I saw all the shopping bags in the hallway, so I'm guessing it's been a good one.'

Just say it, Fern. Tell him what you know and wipe that smirk off his face.

'So, what did you buy?' he asks as he opens the fridge and removes the orange juice carton before taking a swig from it.

I'd normally tell him off for drinking straight from the carton rather than pouring it into a glass, but somehow that indiscretion doesn't seem very important in the grand scheme of things. It's certainly not the worst thing he's done recently, but why haven't I said anything yet? And why does it feel like the longer I leave it, the less chance there is of me actually doing it?

'Hello, is there anybody in there?' Drew says with a laugh after I've failed to respond to him.

'Huh?'

'I asked you what you bought today. Anything nice?'

'Erm, no, not really. Just a few bits.'

'Like what?'

'Erm, just a couple of tops. Nothing much.'

'Wow, this is the least enthusiastic I've ever seen you be about shopping.'

He laughs again before swigging from the carton one more time, and I want to do it, I really do, but I realise that I can't. For some reason, it feels easier and safer to keep up the charade than to be honest. I guess Drew already knows that himself with what he's been doing all this time.

There's also an aspect of this that makes me feel like not saying it out loud makes it less real, as if I can pretend it isn't true. At the moment, I'm only at war with my thoughts, and maybe that's better than verbalising those thoughts and actually being at war with Drew.

I wonder if Rory has been more successful with speaking to his partner. We swapped numbers just before he left my house so I could message him and ask him how it went. I suppose it only needs one of us to bite the bullet and confront our respective partners, because once one of them knows that the game is up then they will surely tell the other. It might be weak of me, but I feel like I'd rather wait for Rory to do the dirty work. Then Alice can tell Drew, saving me the unpleasantness of bringing it up myself.

Drew is too distracted with his phone to notice me on mine, so I text Rory and ask for an update. But when I get it, it appears he hasn't got any further than me:

I tried, but I couldn't do it

I admit I was the same. Then we arrange to meet, both in need of support to try and find our way through this mess. The next day, when Drew is back at work, and Alice is otherwise occupied, I meet Rory in a bar in the city.

When I see him, he looks like he got about as much sleep as I did the previous night, which is none at all.

'It was harder than I thought it would be,' I tell him as we sit in a corner booth, nursing a couple of drinks. 'I tried to just blurt it out, but it was impossible. And do you know what the worst thing was? The whole time I was wrestling with that, my husband was swanning around our kitchen without a care in the world.'

'I know what you mean,' Rory admits before taking a nervous gulp of his whiskey. 'Alice had no idea what I was trying to tell her. She was so calm, so relaxed. I think seeing how easily she can be two-faced is what's made this whole thing even worse.'

We're both in agreement that the thing that hurts the most here is not just the cheating itself, but the continued confidence with which the pair of them are carrying on with their lives.

Another round of drinks gets bought, followed by another, and the tipsier we get, the more we enjoy coming up with ways to get back at our cheating partners. But they're all just silly fantasies and ideas rather than serious things that we'd ever think of carrying out, and while we're trying our best to cheer ourselves up, we both know that, eventually, we'll have to do the sensible thing and just end our relationships with our partners.

I end up reflecting on my marriage with Drew and bemoaning how I never thought something like adultery would ever be a thing I'd have to deal with in it. I say how my partner has mostly been nothing but affectionate and attentive during our relationship, from an early date at the cinema when he went to buy me popcorn halfway through the movie, after I'd changed my mind about wanting it, to our honeymoon in the

Caribbean, when he arranged for rose petals to be laid out all over the floor of our suite upon arrival.

Rory has his own tales of Alice being the seemingly perfect partner in the past, before making it clear that his main worry now is about having to start all over again, but with the baggage that comes from being a divorcée now attached to him to take into his next relationship.

We really are a couple of sad souls sitting in the corner of this bar, a bar that empties out gradually until it reaches closing time, and we're the only two people in there. We know our partners will be wondering where we are but, considering what they have done to us, we don't give much of a damn about that. As we stumble outside into the dark Manchester night, both of us are drunk, emotional and feeling in the mood for revenge.

Which might explain why we ended up kissing.

TWENTY-NINE

FERN

PRESENT DAY

I guess it was that kiss outside that bar in Manchester that started all of this. No, wait, that's not true. It was that kiss outside the hotel that preceded it. If Drew and Alice hadn't locked lips in the first instance, Rory and I never would have ended up doing the same thing. It's their fault all of this happened, not ours.

It's Drew's fault he is now dead.

And it's Alice's fault that she has now been officially charged with his murder.

I knew that was the next logical thing to happen after the police had initially arrested her, but I've still had to be patient while they carried out the search of her home. It was a search that was mainly driven by a need for the police to locate her mobile phone, so they could read the messages on it to corroborate them with the messages already seen on Drew's phone. But the fact Alice had told them her phone was missing, something she had also mentioned to me at the coffee morning before

Drew's body was discovered, meant that it wasn't straightforward for the police to get their hands on it.

But they found it easily in the end.

'It was hidden in a shoebox at the back of her wardrobe,' Detective Tomlin tells me.

'What was it doing there?'

'I guess that was where she hid it. She didn't do a very good job.'

'She lied about losing her phone? Why would she do that?'

'Because she obviously didn't want us to see the message on it. But we have, and we've confirmed that she did indeed send your husband a text on the day of his death, telling him to meet her at the beach. The meeting point is the exact place where his body was found.'

'She planned to do it?' I say, disbelieving. 'So, this wasn't just a random thing?'

'It looks like she wanted to get your husband to a quiet spot where nobody could see what she was going to do to him.'

'Has she admitted it now?'

'No, she is still denying everything. Well, almost everything.'

I detect a shift in the detective's demeanour, and he looks uncomfortable, even more so than when discussing my husband's death with me earlier.

'What is it?'

'I'm afraid your husband was involved in a relationship with Alice.'

'What do you mean?'

'They were having an affair.'

'An affair?'

'Yes.'

More acting is required on my part before we continue as I get upset then angry then upset again.

'No. Impossible. Drew would never cheat on me.'

'We have several messages between the pair of them in which it's obvious that they were involved with each other. Alice has admitted they were seeing each other, both here and in Manchester.'

'The affair started in Manchester?'

Detective Tomlin nods sheepishly.

'I don't understand. They knew each other before we met them up here? They just pretended to be strangers?'

'Yes.'

'No, there must be a mistake.'

'I'm afraid not.'

'I don't believe it. You're wrong.'

The detective waits patiently while I process my 'shock' before I say something he can answer a little easier.

'What does Rory say about this? Did he know what was going on?'

'He's just as shocked as you are. It seems they were very good at keeping it a secret.'

'I still don't understand. Even if they were seeing each other in Manchester, what were the chances they would both end up here in the village?'

'We believe your husband followed Alice here.'

'He did *what*?'

It's exhausting having to keep pretending so much, but I have no choice as the detective goes over the things that I already knew.

'Based on the messages we have read on both of their phones, Alice ended the affair in Manchester, but Drew didn't want to let it go. He must have gotten you to move here under false pretences, and then he went about trying to change Alice's mind. Based on their correspondence with each other, it seems she was reluctant at first, but then they began to meet again. Although it's possible that Alice only agreed to meet him once she realised he wasn't leaving her alone, so she planned to take action to stop his harassment of her.'

'Harassment? He was stalking her?'

'Possibly. It would give her motive to harm him if he was.'

'What did she say to that?'

'She denies it. Admits they had started the affair again and that she had met him a few times since he got to the village, but she is adamant that she never sent that last message about meeting by the rocks.'

'Oh, that was good of her to admit to meeting another woman's husband a few times in private,' I snarl sarcastically as I shake my head and clench my fists.

'Do you believe her?' I ask then, my next question important in more ways than one.

'Honestly? No, I don't.'

'Yeah, I mean the message came from her phone, right?'

'Yes, although that doesn't always mean she sent it.'

'Doesn't it?'

'We might need more.'

'Like what?'

'We still haven't recovered the murder weapon yet. Whatever was used to hit Drew over the head is still missing. But we're looking for it as we speak.'

'And if you find it? Is that enough?'

'Let's just take it one step at a time. Alice is in custody, and she won't be going anywhere for a while. If the weapon is in this village then we'll find it. Based on the fact the murder took place at the beach, it's possible the weapon may have been thrown into the sea, and if that is the case, it might never be retrieved.'

'What if it isn't?'

'There's still enough evidence to take Alice to trial. But it's not necessarily conclusive. Just because they were having an affair, it doesn't mean she did it. That text message about the meeting place is key, but a good defence lawyer might still be able to get her out of it.'

'Then you have to find that weapon. I want justice for my husband.'

'I understand.'

I'm being careful not to play the angry, jealous wife after learning of Drew's affair because that would only give me motive to hurt him, and I don't want anybody wondering if I might have found out about his infidelity before I came into this room.

'We'll keep you updated,' Detective Tomlin tells me before we part again, and I return home with my family after that, though it's even more uncomfortable in the house now because Drew's parents are here.

As I presumed they would be, the pair of them are devastated, each looking like they haven't eaten or slept since they received word that their son was dead. I wish I wasn't responsible for putting them through this because they are good people with good morals, unlike their offspring, and they don't deserve this torment. But neither did I, and that's just life, I guess.

They've already been told the latest on the case against Alice and are convinced of her guilt, just like everybody else in this village. The media are reporting her as the villain already, portraying her as a sex-crazed city girl who played a dangerous game with a married man until it got out of hand, and she got violent. It's amazing how journalists can speculate on things and write anything they need to in order to get clicks and reads, but it's a version of events that I am more than happy for them to report. If only they knew what kind of juicy story they were really sitting on, one that might one day be uncovered with just a bit more investigating and a little luck, but they are far too busy writing titillating pieces to think that there might be more to this than meets the eye. Unfortunately, the police aren't quite as easily side-tracked, and despite Detective Tomlin telling me that he thinks Alice is responsible for Drew's murder, there is that outstanding matter of the pesky murder weapon.

Just where might it be?

The fact that the beach is being extensively searched proves where the police believe it to be, and as they keep focusing their efforts there, I occasionally keep watch on their progress from my bedroom window. It's a bedroom that has a hollow feel to it now that I no longer have anybody to share it with. Although that hollow feeling was lurking even while Drew was still alive, because I know that while he might have been present in body with me in the past, his mind was usually elsewhere.

But I'm not just finding myself staring out of the window to watch over the police. I'm doing it because it makes me look like the grieving widow, one who is too upset to go downstairs and sit with everybody else, and one who needs to have some alone time to process all her thoughts. Being up here keeps me away from having to make awkward conversation with Drew's parents, as well as my own, and I'm glad they are leaving me to myself for the most part. Of course, they do come to check on me regularly, if only to make sure that the window is still locked, and I haven't thrown myself out of it yet. But they always find me in my chair gazing out at the beach, and they offer me a drink before closing the door and giving me a little more peace.

I end up falling asleep in that chair a couple of times over the next twenty-four hours, and it's during one of those times when a new update comes through.

The murder weapon has been found.

It was a sniffer dog on the beach who made the vital discovery, digging into the sand until his handler realised he was on to something and coordinated all efforts into that particular area.

It turns out that the instrument used to strike Drew over the head was a shovel, the kind most people keep in their garage or shed for odd jobs around the garden. But this particular shovel was used for much more than gardening, and the DNA from Drew's skull that was found on it was not the only interesting thing for the police. That's because Alice's fingerprints were all over it too.

As far as Detective Tomlin is concerned, this is now a slam-dunk. He and his colleagues believe that Alice lured Drew down to the beach under false pretences, struck him over the head with the shovel until he was dead and then buried the weapon in the sand, believing it would not be discovered. Unfortunately for her it has been, and now despite maintaining her innocence, she faces what is surely going to be a very one-sided murder trial that can only have one outcome.

I'll be in court to witness that trial, as will my family, Drew's family and anybody else who is able to make it into the viewing gallery. Rory will be there too, of course, in his capacity as husband of the accused, a man shellshocked at what his wife was capable of behind his back, or at least that is how the journalists are reporting him. But I know he's not as surprised as he is making out, just like I'm not either. The truth is that we put all of this into motion, and it is working out exactly as we'd hoped.

But we're not the villains here. We haven't taken things too far, despite what Drew and Alice did to us. No, we gave that pair every chance to change their destiny. Rory, in particular, was determined to try and do the right thing and ensure all four of us had a very alternate reality.

We tried.

We really, really tried.

But Drew and Alice failed.

THIRTY

FERN

How is a wife supposed to take living with a cheating husband? Day by day, I guess. That's how I've been taking it ever since I found out about Drew's affair. It's been a couple of weeks since Rory dropped his bombshell on my driveway and turned my whole world upside down. Two weeks of pretending like I'm okay. Two weeks of having to be around Drew and not scream, or hurl abuse, or just drop to my knees and ask him how he could do this to me. A whole fortnight of looking at various photos of us hanging on the walls around the house, wondering how I could have ever been happy enough to smile so widely. It's been horrible, but somehow I've got through it, so much so that I'm starting to wonder if leaving him is even something that has to happen now.

I'm trying to view what he has done with Alice not through the eyes of a scorned woman but through somebody a bit more impartial, and by doing that I can make a case for him. It was a moment of weakness. A lapse in judgement. Maybe he's been stressed at work. Perhaps I haven't been paying him enough attention. Maybe it's something he just needed to get out of his system. Perhaps it was his version of a mid-life crisis. *Boys will be boys.*

I know I'm making excuses for him, and I also know that part of the reason for that is because I'm not entirely innocent myself these days. Not after I shared a kiss with Rory outside the bar that night. Okay, so it wasn't a full-blown affair, but, technically, I'm still a married woman, so I've cheated too. I'm not quite sure it makes us even, and it was only in retaliation to what Drew did before, but it's still proof to me that life isn't as simple as it might seem. People slip up. People do things they shouldn't, things they regret. That doesn't make them bad. It just makes them human.

I'm not the only one who has debated giving their partner another chance. I know that Rory had the same dilemma over what to do with Alice too, and he told me as much when I saw him yesterday. Although, by that point, he had already come to his decision. Rather wisely, we decided to hold this particular meeting in a place that didn't serve copious amounts of alcohol, so there was no danger of the pair of us losing our inhibitions and ending up falling into each other's arms again.

The coffee shop where we met was busy and full of office workers, and it was there that Rory told me his master plan to try and save his marriage and guarantee that his wife's affair with my husband came to an end.

'I suggested to Alice that we move away, and she has agreed to the idea.'

'Move away? Where?'

'Arberness. It's a village up near Scotland. I was actually born there, although my parents moved away when I was young. I've been back a lot over the years, often with Alice, and we both love it up there. It's quiet. Not like here.'

He had gestured to the swarm of people seated all around us in the coffee shop to illustrate his point, but I remember thinking it was almost as if he was blaming the craziness of city life for what his wife had done, which is ridiculous, but I didn't say anything.

'I told Alice that with my job being remote now since the pandemic, we could live anywhere, so it didn't make sense to be paying all this money here when we could move somewhere much more affordable. I wasn't sure she would go for it, but she actually said she liked the sound of it.'

'She still doesn't know that you caught her?'

'No.'

'Are you sure about that? Because maybe she does, and she's just saying what she thinks you want to hear.'

'No, she has no idea I know about her and Drew. I haven't said a word to her about it. I told you, I can't. It's too hard.'

'I know, I'm just checking. So, you think this move will be enough to make her faithful again?'

'I have no idea, but I have to try. I don't want to lose her. I still love her so much, despite what she's done.'

I had nodded then to show Rory that I understood his plight. I knew he was a good man, a genuine man, and I could see why he'd rather explore every avenue to save his marriage before taking the bulldozing approach of asking for a divorce.

'I just think that no good can come from me leaving her. We'd both just be alone then, but this way, if we move, it can be a fresh start for us.'

'I think it's worth a try.'

'You do? You don't think I'm being stupid.'

'No, of course not. You're doing what you think is best for your relationship.'

'I just keep thinking about all the people who came to our wedding day. Imagine having to tell them that the vows they witnessed were all for nothing. I don't want them to feel bad, and I certainly don't want them to feel bad for me. I'd rather they just didn't know, and maybe they don't have to. And everyone deserves a second chance.'

'As long as you're doing it for the right reasons. Stay with her because you love her, not because you're embarrassed to be single again.'

Rory had seemed to understand my point before he broached the rather awkward subject of our kiss.

'I don't mean to offend you or anything but what happened outside that bar made me realise how strongly I still feel about Alice,' he had said. 'I mean, even though I was kissing you, I was still thinking about her.'

'Charming,' I'd replied then, lightening the mood at our table a little.

'You know what I mean. I still have feelings for my wife, strong feelings, so I can't give up on those. Not yet anyway...'

That last sentence had been rather telling, and I knew what Rory had been hinting at. He was hoping the move away would not only be a new start for the couple but see Alice return to her faithful ways. But that wasn't guaranteed.

'Of course, I'll have to monitor her,' Rory had told me solemnly. 'Check her messages. Maybe even follow her occasionally. Otherwise, I guess there will always be a doubt in the back of my mind about what she might be up to and with who.'

'I understand. I guess I'll have to do the same with Drew.'

'So, you're going to stay with him too?'

'I think so. I'm taking it slowly. Maybe I'll change my mind tomorrow, but as of today, yeah, I think I want to stay with him. We have so much history. And so many plans for our future.'

'It's not as easy as they make it seem in the movies, is it? There, when someone catches a cheat, they usually just have a big argument, go their separate ways, meet someone new, end up having lots of sex and hijinks along the way. But real life isn't like that, is it?'

'I don't know what movies you've been watching,' I'd said

with a laugh. 'But yeah, I get what you mean. Real life is very different.'

'At least me moving away with Alice will end this current affair. I doubt they'll try and see each other with such a vast distance involved now. Hopefully this was just a big mistake. A one-off.'

'Yeah, I guess.'

'But you will let me know if you suspect anything is still going on?'

'Of course. And you'll do the same?'

'I promise.'

Such a sombre and sobering conversation inevitably means both of us wear grim expressions as we talk, neither one of us feeling like we have come out on top here, rather we have potentially applied a plaster to a very large wound, and we're just going to hope it sticks and heals in time.

After making our rather grim pact to keep an eye on our partners and inform the other of any issues, it had seemed there wasn't much more for us to talk about. But it was obvious we both found it comforting to be around the other one while we processed all our emotions, so the conversation had continued for a little while longer.

'When do you think you'll move?' I'd asked Rory then.

'Very soon. My aunt has a place up there that sits empty most of the year, so we could move into there. It'll do for the time being until the money from the house sale comes through, then we'll get somewhere sorted.'

'Is your house up for sale yet?'

'No, but that's my next job.'

'Wow, you are moving fast.'

'Yeah. It's amazing how motivated I am when my marriage is on the line,' he had told me, displaying that dark sense of humour that had helped me become fond of him.

'I wonder if Alice is ready for the affair to end? I guess she must be if she's wanting to go as quickly as you.'

'Possibly. Maybe she knows it's for the best if she gets away. Stop playing with fire, so to speak.'

'I hope Drew is happy for it to end too. I guess it'll be hard for me to know.'

'Try not to think like that. Just focus on each day, like you said.'

'Yeah.'

The conversation petered out quickly after that, and it was funny how we had very little to talk about beyond our partners' affair. As we said our goodbyes outside the coffee shop, we shared a warm hug, one that was reflective of two people who wished they had never had to meet but knew the other was just trying their best.

That was yesterday, and I guess by now, if he's stuck to his word, Rory has put his house up for sale. That means Alice really is going to be leaving this city. I wonder if she has broken the news to Drew yet.

I'll be watching his mood closely over the next few weeks. If it's good, I guess he never really cared about her. If it's bad, then maybe he's taking it harder than I would have liked. As with all things, time will tell. But I can't help feeling cautiously optimistic about the future. I can only wish Rory all the best up north in his new life, while hoping for the best for me back here.

I'm not quite sure I could ever make the move to a place so different to the city, but he obviously likes it up there, and if circumstances were different, it would be good to stop off there and say hello to him if Drew and I were ever passing through on our way for a short break in Scotland. In an alternate reality, I'm sure all four of us could have been friends. But obviously that is never going to happen. I need to keep Drew as far away from that village as possible, and it shouldn't be too hard because it's over two hundred miles away. All I need to worry about now is making sure Drew doesn't start a new relationship with someone else in Manchester because, if he does, then I won't be able to forgive and forget a second time.

I'm not quite sure what I'll do if I ever catch him cheating again, but I do know one thing.

It won't be pretty.

THIRTY-ONE

FERN

The trial of Alice Richardson began on a rainy spring day, and the bleak mood outside the courtroom was reflected inside it. There were no smiles as the members of the jury took their seats. No smiles from the lawyers for the prosecution and the defence, nor a smile from the judge as they appeared to oversee proceedings. And there were certainly no smiles in the viewing gallery, which is where I was seated, only a couple of places away from Rory, as we prepared to watch his estranged wife face the music for the murder of my husband.

Being one of only two people in the courtroom who knew the truth about what had really happened to Drew Devlin, Rory and I made sure to keep our interactions to a minimum. Not courting attention or suspicion, but simply carrying ourselves like two people who had been dealt a very bad hand in life, who were here to get some form of closure from the law before they could make the necessary steps to move on.

Despite trying to stay composed, I couldn't help but gasp when I first saw Alice appear to take her place in the dock. Her time in police custody had not been kind to her, and it was obvious she had lost weight, colour and any kind of zest for life during that time. The stress and enormity of the situation, as well as the injustice of it, of course, was clearly taking its toll on her, and she looked exhausted as she spoke to confirm her name, her address and, most importantly, her plea.

It was still 'not guilty'.

And it was still going to take a miracle for a jury to agree with her.

The first part of the trial saw the prosecution state their case, and this was where everything I had carefully set in motion was unveiled, the jury being enlightened as to a sordid tale of extra-marital affairs, new starts in a quiet village and, ultimately, a dangerous liaison on the beach after dark, all told with the help of several text messages between the accused and the victim.

It was during the prosecution's work that I knew Alice was doomed. Not only was the KC tasked with putting her behind bars clearly excellent at his job, but the jury could surely not screw up so badly and dismiss all this evidence that was being presented to them. And, for her part, Alice appeared like she knew she was fighting a losing battle. Gone was the anger and desperation with which she professed her innocence when she was initially arrested. In its place was a quiet resignation that somehow, some way, she had been set up.

She was right, of course, because she had been set up, but, thankfully, she hadn't figured out how. She hadn't guessed that Rory might have had something to do with it, and she certainly hadn't pointed the finger of blame at me at any point. It was as if she was completely baffled as to how this could have happened, and rather than trying to work it out until she eventually stumbled upon the right answer, she had become overwhelmed and worn down, probably not helped by the rumours that her lawyers had spent considerable time trying to get her to change her plea in the hope of a more lenient sentence.

Could there be anything more soul-destroying than being accused of a crime that you didn't commit, and not even the people tasked with keeping you out of prison believe you? I imagine not. I also imagine that Alice has spent every one of her days in custody reflecting on her actions and how she wouldn't be here if she hadn't gotten involved with Drew.

What did she like about the affair? The thrill? The unpredictability? The fact she was getting away with something that nobody else knew about?

Well, all I can say is that now I know exactly how she feels.

It's a week into the trial before the defence get to have their say, and I don't envy the barrister tasked with persuading the jury that Alice is innocent of all she has been accused of over the past several days. But there's a reason lawyers get paid well, and that's because they're expected to do things that not everybody can. They give it a damn good go, doing all they can to poke holes in the police's version of events, finding ways to instil doubt into the jury's mind.

I've found myself watching and studying the faces of the jury members a lot during the trial, not only because what they decide will determine whether or not my overall plan has been a success, but because it's curiously fascinating to see twelve strangers thrown together and effectively holding the fate of another stranger in their hands. I've never been selected for jury duty myself, nor would I want to be, because it's a role that carries great responsibility. They are the ones who have to listen to both sides of a compelling argument and then decide which side they believe the most, but there is always the chance they could be wrong.

No pressure then.

The jury members themselves are a mix of ages, ranging from their twenties to their sixties, and presumably they all come from different backgrounds and have different life experiences that make up who they are, which will go some way into shaping their decisions here. Some might find themselves subconsciously feeling unsympathetic towards the accused, while secretly despising her and just counting down to the moment when they get to give their verdict. Preconceived notions are a real thing, and there's no point denying it. They're all supposed to be impartial people, but I'm not sure how that is possible when life isn't impartial. Nothing and nobody in this life is equal, and I don't know how anybody can pretend that it is. All of this feels like a charade, a performance for the judge to preside over, but I guess that's no different to what Rory and I have been doing for all this time.

After the tense, awkward and rather depressing trial has run its course, eventually, the judge sends the jury members away to consider their verdicts.

There's a welcome break in the torrid, unseasonable weather on the day that the verdict is due, and as I make my way up the steps of the courthouse beneath a clear blue sky, a cold wind whips around me, yet I feel comfortingly warmed by the knowledge that this will be over soon. This is the last step in things that have to happen. Alice will hopefully go to prison, and the case will be closed, allowing the police to move on and allowing me to do the same thing. It will be a chance to remember what life was like before I became consumed by the need for revenge, before I had to spend every waking minute of my day pretending to be somebody that I'm not. No longer will I have to be the naïve spouse or the grieving widow, or the shocked citizen who can't believe such violence could occur right under her nose. Instead, I'll get to be plain old Fern again, and I can't wait.

'Have you reached a verdict upon which you are agreed?'

The eyes of the courtroom are on the jury foreman as they respond positively.

'On the charge of murder, how do you find the defendant?'

It seems to take an age for a response, but in reality it's just a mere second.

'Guilty.'

Alice's head drops. Mine does too, but for a very different reason. She's devasted, while I'm relieved. Now all that is left to do is hear the sentencing. It seems that someone is unable to. Rory is making his way out of the gallery. As he goes, he steals a glance at me. I have no idea what he is doing, but I wish he had just stayed where he was and not drawn attention to himself. I suppose it could look like he is just distressed about seeing the woman he married be found guilty of a heinous crime, and him needing some fresh air to process it all. That's fine if everybody else thinks that's what it is. But I'm thinking the enormity of what he and I have done has just hit him after the guilty verdict was reached, and now I'm worried that he might not be able to hold it together.

But I'm not so foolish as to leave my seat and go after him. I stay where I am until the judge has had their say. By the time they have, Alice has been sentenced to twenty years behind bars, and as she's led away she looks up at the seat where Rory once sat. But he's long gone, and that's my next move.

The last obstacle to overcome is answering a couple of questions from the journalists outside the courthouse, several of whom want to know how I feel about a verdict being reached in the murder of my husband.

'I am glad justice has been done, but there are no winners here. I would like to be left alone to get on with my life now, thank you.'

And with that, I make my exit, climbing into the back of a car along with my parents, before we make the drive back to the village and the home that I will soon be listing for sale. I told everybody that I was planning to go back to Manchester, but I couldn't think about that until the court case was over. Now that it is, it's time to leave the village behind.

It's funny, but despite everything that has happened, it only feels like yesterday when Drew suggested we move here.

A suggestion that turned out to be the worst idea of his life.

THIRTY-TWO

FERN

SIX MONTHS AGO

With Rory and Alice having already left Manchester, I've been keeping a close eye on Drew, to gauge his moods. As I feared, it hasn't been good. He seems to be missing Alice, or at least that's the only explanation I have for him being grumpy, irritable and occasionally aggressive with the way he speaks to me on several occasions over these past few weeks.

It seems like every little thing gets on his nerves these days, from the dishwasher to the recycling to the squeaky bathroom door. I'm so used to him stomping up and down the stairs every night after he gets home from work that I don't even bother asking him about his day anymore, and I've become so accustomed to him drinking far more than he should on the weekends that I don't ask him to slow down or tell him I'm worried he might have a problem. That's because I know what his problem is, and it's not a bad day at work or an alcohol dependency or anything like that.

It's because Alice has gone, and he is forced to just make do with me again.

For all the hoping that her moving away might bring Drew closer to me again, it's become painfully obvious that it hasn't worked. I find myself wondering how Rory has been getting on up north, and interested to know if Alice is displaying any of the tendencies that Drew is. Eventually, my curiosity gets the better of me and I reach out to Rory to ask him for an update, calling him one night while Drew is sat out in the back garden, swigging from yet another bottle of beer and staring rather mournfully at the flowerbeds.

'Fern, hi. How are you? Is everything okay?'

It's actually quite pleasant to hear Rory's voice again, or maybe it's just been a while since I had a man ask me how I was. God knows the last time Drew enquired about such a thing.

'I'm not sure. It's Drew. He's not been himself since you left. I think he misses Alice.'

'Oh, I see.'

'I was wondering how Alice has been. Have you noticed a change in her since you moved up there?'

'Yes, I have actually, but it's been a positive one. She's been more attentive with me. More present. I'm sorry to hear that you are having problems with Drew, but as far as Alice is concerned, she's been fine.'

'I'm glad to hear it,' I say, and I genuinely mean it because I'm happy for Rory. It sounds like his marriage is back on track again, so the move away hasn't been a waste of time. But it has shown me how much my husband cared for Alice, and it's obvious it was about far more than just sex, at least for him anyway.

'So, you don't think they're still in touch somehow?' I ask Rory before I let him go, expecting him to just say no and that will be the end of it. But he hesitates to answer me, and I get the feeling there's something he doesn't want to tell me.

'What is it?' I ask him as I look out of my kitchen window at

Drew sitting in the garden, absent-mindedly peeling the label off his beer bottle.

'I have occasionally been checking Alice's phone while she has been asleep, and I'm afraid that Drew has messaged her a couple of times, using private messages on social media.'

'Saying what?'

He hesitates again, but I urge him to tell me everything, no matter how painful it might be.

'He says he misses her. Wishes she had never left. Says he's not sure how he can go on without her.'

It's nothing more than I had already gathered from his behaviour, but hearing it like that is like a punch to the stomach. As if he could say those things to another woman.

'I see.'

'I'm sorry, Fern.'

'Has she been messaging him back?'

'Only once. She told him that they had to both move on and that he was to stop contacting her. He hasn't listened to that, but she hasn't replied since.'

It seems like Rory is the lucky one in all this. His partner has come to her senses, while mine is still acting like a man without any morals.

'Okay, thank you for telling me this,' I say before I end the call, glad I made it but devastated at what I ended up hearing.

It's at this point that I decided enough is enough. I'm going to end this. I'm going to walk out into the garden and take a seat beside him and I will tell him how I feel. I'll tell him that I have sensed a distance growing between us over these past few months and that, after giving it some serious thought, I have decided that the best thing for us to do is separate.

I wonder if he will even fight it or just agree. Whatever he says, I am determined to stick to my decision.

But when I do, he goes and says the one thing I was not expecting.

'I hear what you're saying and you're right,' Drew tells me after I have just raised the idea of us splitting up. 'We have been growing apart recently and I take the blame for that. I've been distant with you. Work's been hard and I'm tired and stressed, but that's no excuse. I should have been making more of an effort.'

It's still not the truth, but at least he's acknowledging how he has been failing me.

'I don't want to lose you, Fern, so I've been thinking. What if we move out of Manchester? Go somewhere new. Somewhere less hectic. Somewhere I could work fewer hours and be home earlier.'

I already know where he is going to suggest before he says it, but I hold out hope he might surprise me and pick somewhere random, like a town or city down south. But no, of course not. He suggests Arberness, and that is the moment I know he is never going to choose me over Alice. Worse than that, he is prepared to keep on lying to me. If he'd genuinely cared about me, he would've just agreed to end our sham marriage. Instead, he's too selfish to think about anyone but himself.

'I'll think about it,' I tell Drew and he seems happy enough with that answer for now, no doubt too giddy about the prospect of being near Alice again that he hasn't paused to consider why I might feel like agreeing to such a drastic thing. If he only stopped and thought about it, he'd know I'd never seriously want to leave Manchester, but, as has been the case in recent times, he isn't thinking about me.

While he goes inside to start plotting the logistics of such a move, I make another phone call to Rory, and he's surprised to hear from me so soon after our last chat. He's even more surprised when I tell him the news.

'He wants to move here? But he can't! You have to stop him!'

'I'm not sure I can.'

'Of course you can. You're his wife. Just tell him you want to stay there. He won't move without you.'

'What good will that do me? I'll just be stuck with him like he is now and he's not happy.'

'That's not my problem! But you coming here is!'

'What's the matter? I thought you trusted Alice again?'

'I do!'

'So why are you so concerned about Drew being around her?'

'Because it's tempting fate! It's stupid!'

'Is it? Or is it the only way we'll ever know for sure if their relationship is over?'

'So, you want to put it to the test by having them live close together again? Are you insane?'

'No, not insane, I'm just fed up. Fed up with being lied to. Fed up with being second best. Fed up with being the one who gets taken for a fool. I want to do something else.'

'Like what?'

'I don't know. All I know is I still can't trust Drew and, for all you say, deep down, you probably know you still can't trust Alice. So how about we put them to the test? It's the only way we'll ever have peace of mind again.'

'And what if it fails? What if they start the affair again? Where does that leave us?'

'It leaves us with no choice but to get our own back.'

'What does that mean?'

'If they do nothing then they will be fine. But if they do something then they will be punished.'

'We leave them?'

'We do more than that.'

I glance back at the house then and see Drew is coming back outside, a bottle of champagne and two glasses in his hand. He looks like he's in a celebratory mood, and I bet he is because he thinks he'll be back with Alice soon enough. I'll have a glass with him because, just like him, I have a secret that I might be getting away with.

'I've got to go,' I tell Rory, before I hang up and put my phone away, just in time to receive a glass from my husband.

'I thought we could have a drink while we plot out the next part of our lives,' Drew says before getting to work on opening the bottle.

'That's an excellent idea,' I reply as he pulls the cork out and pours me a hearty measure. 'Here's to plotting.'

THIRTY-THREE

FERN

PRESENT DAY

It's only now that everything has played out that I can look back and admire my work.

After agreeing to move to the village with Drew, and despite Rory's protests that it was not a good idea, I was genuinely willing to give both my husband and Alice a chance. Of course, I knew I'd see Rory in the village and that the pair of us would have to pretend not to know the other one, but that was pretty easy to do. The hard part came when it was becoming obvious that the affair had started again, because that was when I knew Rory had been right. Those two could not be trusted around each other.

We had played with fire.

And now somebody was going to get burned.

I was determined that it wasn't going to be me, so I concocted a plan in which both Drew and Alice would pay, while Rory and I would get our revenge without suffering any consequences. The first part of that plan involved Rory taking his wife's phone and sending Drew a message, posing as Alice, in which she told him to meet at the rocks on the beach. Then, when he was there, and after I had confronted him, Rory crept out of his hiding place and struck Drew over the head with a shovel, one that had Alice's fingerprints on it, after Rory had cunningly asked her to help him in the garden a couple of days before, killing him instantly before burying the weapon in the sand, far enough away from the body so that it wouldn't be found easily, but close enough so that the police would be able to locate it eventually.

But killing Drew wouldn't have been much good without a plan for Alice, as well as a plan to keep the two of us out of prison, so we had made sure to have all our bases covered there. Along with the text in which it seemed that Alice had arranged the meeting with Drew, Rory made sure to keep hold of her phone long enough for her to think that she had lost it. That way, she could genuinely tell the police that she couldn't hand over her device to them when they asked to see it after discovering her message on Drew's mobile. Rory had merely hidden the phone in their house, and despite putting up a very convincing display at the police station in which he tried to refuse the police access to his home while Alice was in custody, he always wanted them to go and look. And, of course, they did, because an angry husband is not going to get in the way of them searching for vital evidence.

I'd like to say that the hardest part of this whole thing was carrying out the actual plan itself, but in hindsight it was rather easy. The most difficult thing had been to convince Rory that this was what we needed to do, because I simply could not have done any of this without him. But that was no simple task.

After seeing Drew and Alice together in his surgery, I had called Rory on my spare phone, one of the two that the pair of us had bought to converse with each other because it seemed safer that way than using our old ones, like we had in the past. On that call, I broke the sad news to him that his wife was up to her old tricks with my husband again. As expected, he was devastated. He also tried to blame me. Saying this would never have happened if I hadn't moved here with Drew, but I reminded him that it would most likely have happened again whatever I had done, because it was obvious by then that Drew needed Alice and wasn't going to give up on her that easily. And it hadn't taken much for Alice to run back into Drew's arms.

While Rory was distraught, he wasn't really in the right frame of mind to think about getting his revenge. I made sure to tell him that I had a plan and that I was ready to carry it out just as soon as he was ready. This was the part I knew was crucial because, if he said no, then all I would have been left with would have been to leave Drew, and that would have been letting him off lightly. Fortunately, I'd already suggested to Rory that we try something, just to prove more to him than to me how devious my husband could really be.

Aware that Drew coveted Alice so much, it only made sense that he would view Rory as a rival. He never made it known publicly, of course, but it had to be how he felt secretly. With that in mind, I suggested Rory visit Drew posing as a patient and relay some rather troubling symptoms, to see how the good doctor would respond to that. If Drew was genuine and could put his professional duties above his jealously of Rory, then he would give his patient the best care he could, referring him quickly and helping him seek out as quick a diagnosis as possible. But if, as I suspected, Drew was tempted to take his chance to remove Rory from the picture, he would provide inadequate treatment and delay the progress of his patient's case.

Still trying to believe that my husband was capable of change, Rory agreed to go along with this and faked an illness, talking about weight loss and stomach pains and a false history of cancer in his family, all things that should have set alarm bells ringing in Drew's head.

And what did Drew do?

Nothing.

Rory knew that because despite calling the nearest hospital and asking about the progress of his referral, they had no news on it, and they had no news because they hadn't received anything from the doctor who had seen him. Rory knew then how far Drew was willing to go to have Alice all to himself. He was willing to delay a patient's care, potentially increasing his chances of death, simply for his own selfish gain, and that was the point when Rory told me he was in on my plan. After all, if Drew had been willing to let Rory die, why would Rory not be willing to do the same?

Explaining how we could do it and get away with it, Rory was helpful enough to pick holes in my plan until it was bullet-proof, and then it was time to act. Now what's done is done, our second phones were tossed into the sea moments after Drew's death, ensuring we couldn't be linked, and all that is left now is for both of us to have to deal with the consequences of our actions. Thankfully, we'll be dealing with them on the outside while Alice deals with hers on the inside.

Now there's only one thing left for me to do, and that is to pack up and leave this place. I've got my parents helping me out with that, and despite it only feeling like yesterday since this house was full of boxes that needed unpacking, it is now begin-ning to fill up with boxes that will be loaded onto a removals truck and driven down to Manchester.

Even after what I've done, I still get strange moments of what I can only call 'fortunate amnesia'. In those moments, I very briefly forget what I did and even that Drew is gone, and while they are extremely fleeting when they come, they do come surprisingly often. The latest one involved me trying to lift a box in the spare bedroom only to struggle with the weight of it. I was just about to call out for Drew to come and give me some help when I remembered.

I guess he'll never truly leave me, even though he is gone,

because we spent so many years together, and his life is forever intertwined with mine, even in death.

As the packing progresses, I'm wondering whether or not to make a quick trip out to say a few goodbyes to some of the people who I knew here, people who were always nice to me but even more so in the aftermath of all that has occurred. People like Audrey, the other women at the coffee morning including Agatha, and a few others like those in the butchers and in the pub. People who lived very normal, ordinary and peaceful lives until I came here and managed to turn their village into what will one day merely end up being just another episode on a true crime series on late-night television. It would be nice of me to show my face one last time, let them know that while this village will forever be tarnished for me now, it has absolutely nothing to do with any of them.

I'm also tempted to take the easy way out and just leave without all the fuss and attention. Go now with my parents. Follow the removals van down the motorway. And never look back. That is until the decision is taken out of my hands by my parents, suggesting we take a short walk into the village just to clear our heads before the long drive back. I reluctantly agree, and we set off for what I expect to be a quick detour before I never set foot in this place again.

But as this village has a habit of doing, it surprises me one last time.

THIRTY-FOUR

FERN

'We don't have time for a drink. I'd rather just get going,' I say to my dad after he's suggested we call in the pub for a refreshment during our walk.

'We've got a long drive ahead of us. I need a pint before facing those motorways,' he tells me, pushing open the door and going inside.

'Come on, we won't be long,' Mum tells me, taking his side even though she's never been much of a drinker herself. As she leads me into the pub, I start to get the feeling that something else might be going on here. And, sure enough, I find out that it is.

Despite it being the middle of the afternoon, the pub is surprisingly busy, and it very quickly becomes obvious why that is. Everyone has come out to bid me farewell, and while it's not quite a leaving party, because a party would be inappropriate after what's happened, it is definitely a gathering of sorts, and it's all for me.

'What's going on?' I ask my parents, who were obviously in on this, whatever this is.

'Everybody just wanted to give you a good memory of this

place before you left,' Mum tells me, her face a picture of sorrow for all that I have lost since I've been here.

'Here you go, Fern, this one's on the house,' the landlord says, coming out from behind the bar to hand me a glass of white wine, and I thank him before smiling at the sea of faces around me, to show my appreciation for them thinking of me before I left. But amongst the faces is somebody who I would prefer to keep my distance from, and that is Rory. He's standing by the bar with a pint of beer in hand, although it doesn't look like it's his first of the day. He raises his glass when he sees me look in his direction, but there's something about the way he looks at me that troubles me.

'I'm so sorry for everything you've been through.'

The voice behind is recognisable as Audrey's, and I turn around just in time for her to embrace me in a warm hug. 'I wish you weren't leaving, but I understand that you feel like you have to go. But I do hope that one day you might feel like visiting and, if you do, make sure you come and see me, okay?'

The genuine goodwill from this woman actually breaks through my defences for a moment, and I feel on the verge of tears, tears that aren't faked like so many of the ones I've shed over the past few months. If Audrey or anyone else in this pub really knew who I was and what I'd done, then they'd never be this kind towards me, but because they don't, they are treating my departure from their village like it's a shame when, in reality, they should be rejoicing. Seeing the back of me will mean an end to the trouble that has befallen this place.

'Thank you so much, Audrey. It was lovely to meet you, and I'll never forget how kind you have been to me ever since I got here. Remember the lasagne you made me?'

'Of course, dear. It was no trouble at all. I only wish that I would one day have got to deliver a meal that wasn't just for you or your partner but a little one as well.'

Audrey means well, but she panics a little when she realises she might have said the wrong thing and apologises.

'It's okay,' I tell her. 'That would have been lovely. But it was not meant to be, I'm afraid.'

I manage to extract myself from Audrey's clutches after a while and spend a little time mingling in the pub, accepting a few more platitudes and saying several more goodbyes, before I eventually make my way over to where Rory is standing at the bar.

'Goodbye, Rory,' I say to him, opening up my arms to give him a hug because that's what two people who had met here and become friends would most likely do before parting. Rory knows not to do anything that might arouse suspicion here, so he accepts my hug, and I wish him all the best, something I really mean because we've been through so much together, and he deserves to be happy again one day. But just before we separate, he whispers in my ear.

'I need to talk to you in private. Meet me around the back of the pub in five minutes.'

I detect the heavy scent of alcohol on his breath, but that's only one of the things that troubles me as I leave him and move on to the next person.

What does he want to talk to me about? Is he having regrets about what we did? If so, it's more than a little late for that. Or is he worried there might be something that could see us get caught out by the police, a track we failed to cover despite trying our best? I don't know, but the anxiety is unbearable as I keep moving around the pub, giving and receiving a few more hugs before I see Rory making his way to the door.

'I'll be right back,' I tell my dad as I hand him my empty wine glass. 'Could you get me another one of those?'

Him going to the bar with Mum should keep them busy enough for the next few minutes so they don't come outside looking for me. As I step outside, I wish I'd never come to this damn pub. I could be in a car on the motorway now with my head back against the seat, trying to get some sleep. Instead, I'm still in this damn village having to deal with whatever Rory wants to tell me, and the longer I'm here, the more I feel like a character in one of those movies where they find themselves unable to escape the place, as if the place is a character in and of itself.

'Hey,' Rory says as he sees me wander around the back of the pub. He's standing over by a pile of empty beer kegs, and he's swaying slightly, clearly inebriated but not looking like he cares too much about that.

'What's going on?'

'I wanted to talk to you before you left. I sent you a message on your second phone, but you never replied.'

'I threw that phone away months ago. You were supposed to have done the same.'

'I guess I hung on to it.'

'Why would you do that? If anybody else found it then it holds evidence that could be used to ruin us.'

'I know. I'm sorry.'

'What the hell is wrong with you? How much have you had to drink?'

'That doesn't matter.'

'It does if there's a chance you might end up talking to some-body about what we did!'

'Give me some credit. I'm not that stupid.'

I realise that I might be being a little harsh to my accom-plice, so I apologise.

'What is this about? What do you want to tell me? Is it about Alice and the trial? Have the police been asking you more questions?'

I'm terrified that they might be on to him and by him, I mean *us*. What mistake did we make? What loose end did we fail to tie up? I should have known getting away with murder wouldn't be as easy as this.

'No, nothing like that,' Rory says, to my enormous relief, and I figure he should be pleased about that too, although he still doesn't look very happy about things.

'Good. Then what is it?'

'I love you.'

'What?'

Of all the things he could have said, that might be the last thing I was expecting.

'You heard me. I've fallen for you, Fern.'

'What the hell are you talking about?'

'I know it's not ideal, but I can't help how I feel. After everything we've been through together, I can't stop thinking about you. That kiss we shared in Manchester. How you refused to let me settle with Alice when you believed she was still no good for me. And what we have been able to do. We're a great team, right?'

'We're just friends. Friends who were unfortunately brought together because of what our partners did.'

'But we're more than that. You kissed me too, remember?'

'I was drunk! Kind of like how you are now!'

Rory looks a little hurt by that, but he also knows it's the truth.

'That kiss was a long time ago. If you had feelings for me then why didn't you say anything?'

'I didn't have feelings then. They've just developed.'

'You're just feeling lonely because Alice is in prison. But you'll be okay. You'll meet somebody else.'

'Who? Who am I going to meet? There's hardly any women my age here, and those who are are already married.'

'Then move.'

'I could come back to Manchester with you?'

'Are you crazy? How do you think that would look? The

pair of us getting together after what happened to Drew and Alice. Talk about suspicious!'

'So, you're saying you don't feel anything towards me?'

'No, I don't and, even if I did, I wouldn't do anything about it because it's far too risky.'

I want to leave and end this nonsensical conversation, but before I go, I need proof that Rory isn't going to do anything to jeopardise things.

'Are we okay?' I ask him, hoping we can leave on good terms rather than awkward ones, because the last thing I need when I get back to Manchester is to worry about what Rory might be saying to someone in a pub the next time he has too much to drink. Surely he wouldn't be so stupid as to blurt out the truth, a truth that could land him in prison just as quickly as me, but the fact I'm still here means it's a worry.

'No, we're not okay,' he tells me rather abruptly. 'I've lost everything. I wish we had never done it. I wish Drew was still alive and Alice was still here with me.'

'Even though they were laughing at us behind our backs?'

'Was that any worse than this? Being alone. Feeling guilty. Having nothing.'

'Pull yourself together! You need to snap out of this. I suggest you go home, sober up and then figure out what you want to do next. But I'm leaving. Goodbye, Rory.'

I turn to walk away, but Rory says possibly the only thing that could get me to stop then.

'I'll tell someone what we did,' he says. 'I'll tell someone unless you admit that kiss meant something to you because I know it did.'

Oh my God, this is really happening. *All this work and effort, and despite getting rid of both Drew and Alice, Rory has ended up being my biggest threat.*

'Rory, you need to let me go. It'll be easier to move on without me around. We'll only remind each other of them.'

'But something good has to come out of all this, doesn't it? Otherwise, what was the point? Just revenge? Isn't there more to life than that?'

'What do you want me to do, Rory? Stay here and be with you, because that's ridiculous, and you know it! So what? Tell me!'

Rory looks at a loss for words for a moment before he finally thinks of a response.

'Come back to mine before you go. I want to be with you. A one-off. Then I'll move on and never say a word to anybody about what we did.'

Is he really doing this? Is he blackmailing me into sleeping with him? It sure sounds that way. I don't know what to say to that. I'm disgusted and dismayed and, in my mind, he's almost as bad as our ex-partners. But he is deadly serious, and now he has made his mind up, I don't seem to have much of a choice.

'If we do this, you promise that it will be the end of it? You won't try and contact me again or come after me? And you won't talk to anybody about what we did?'

'No, I promise.'

I shake my head and show him that there isn't much else I can do then.

'Fine,' I tell him. 'You go home, and I'll meet you there in ten minutes. I just need to make an excuse in the pub.'

Rory has a stupid grin on his face as he heads for his house, while I go back into the pub, my head swimming over what just happened, but I don't have time for anything other than telling my parents that I need to go and do something before we leave the village.

'I want to take a walk on the beach. By myself. Say goodbye to Drew one last time.'

I hope it's a good enough story for them to leave me alone while I go to Rory's and, thankfully, they understand.

'Take as much time as you need, love,' Dad says before

giving me a hug. 'We'll meet you back at the house when you're ready to go.'

'I love you, darling,' Mum says as she hugs me too. 'I'm so proud of you and how brave you are being.'

I thank both my parents before leaving the pub. As I head in the direction of Rory's place, I give myself a little pep talk.

'Just get this over with,' I say to myself as I walk through the quiet streets. 'It won't be fun, but at least it will be the last thing I ever have to do in this damn village.'

THIRTY-FIVE

FERN

ONE MONTH LATER

They say you never really leave a place you love because you'll always carry a part of it with you wherever you go. I guess that's true, because Manchester never left me, even when I was in that village surrounded by nothing but empty streets and acres of empty sand.

Even while I was there, I would always think back to the busy alleyways of the city and the people who would rush through them on their way to a high-rise office, a museum or a pub, or the latest showing of a big-scale production at the theatre. Instead of the sea air by the coast, I would occasionally remember what it was like to get a waft of coffee in my nostrils as I walked past a place where skilled baristas expertly poured milk into cups, making pretty pictures on the surface of what could have easily just been a plain beverage. How could I forget the wine bars, those decadently decorated venues where one was always made to feel at home, whether they were coming inside out of the rain for a single glass before catching their train home, or occupying a table for several hours with several friends, a bottle between them and nowhere else to be.

Out of everything, it was those kinds of places I missed the most, so I guess that explains why, on my first night back out enjoying the city since my move home, I am sitting at a bar on a Friday night and savouring every single second of the activity going on around me.

I came here by myself, and I'm not planning on talking to anybody, but that doesn't mean that I feel alone as I engage in a little people-watching. There's no better place than this for such a game, and as I look around at the patrons who I share this venue with, I make up all sorts of silly stories about them in my head.

There's the guy in the flowery shirt and shorts who I imagine is a surfer dude from California, who has somehow ended up here on the rain-soaked streets of Manchester and has been trying to find his way home ever since. There's the large lady in the yellow dress who keeps spilling champagne on her table, and I imagine she is a lucky lottery winner who is blowing through her fortune quickly before she ends up back where she started, penniless and having to pawn off that pretty dress for a bit of cash. Then there's the suave guy standing near me at the bar, with his dreamy blue eyes and rugged jawline, and I imagine he is a model who has just got the night off, he's out celebrating another six-figure contract with an aftershave company who will put his face on a billboard in Times Square very soon.

As I stare at him and lose myself in my silly daydream, I fail to realise that he is staring right back at me.

By the time I snap out of it, the stranger has clearly got the impression that I am interested, because he confidently sidles up beside me and tells me he couldn't help but notice I was paying him some attention.

'Oh, I'm sorry,' I say, feeling embarrassed. 'I was daydreaming. I didn't mean to stare.'

'Or you didn't mean to get caught?'

He gives me a cheeky wink and puts me at ease before asking me if I'm enjoying my evening.

'Yeah, it's been good so far.'

'Are you by yourself or waiting for a date?'

'Yeah, I'm waiting for a hunky, gorgeous guy to get here and buy me another drink,' I jest.

'Well, I'm here now, so what can I get you?' he replies without skipping a beat, and I laugh loudly, although much of it is drowned out by the loud music in here, which I'm quite grateful for.

I consider my options, aware that just because I'm being hit on by a cute guy, it doesn't mean I have to lead him on and potentially get myself involved in something. I could just make polite small talk for a little while and then leave, pretending that I have to get back home because somebody is waiting for me there, a husband perhaps, and the wedding ring on my left hand would help make that story more believable.

I'm still wearing the ring that Drew slid onto my finger on our wedding day, even after his death and all that he did to me. While I am looking forward to the day when I can take it off permanently, so that it doesn't have to act as a constant reminder of him, I have kept it on for now, so I still look like the sad widow who longs for what she once had. Even after all this time and even with another woman in prison for his murder, I am still being sensible, and making sure nobody suspects me.

But a girl does get lonely being by herself after a while, which is why I don't feel like I want to end this conversation just yet. It's nice to talk and flirt, especially with a guy as cute as this one, so when he tells me he is serious about wanting to get me another drink, I accept his kind offer and allow him to take the empty seat beside me.

'So, are you really waiting for somebody or are you all alone tonight?' he asks me as the bartender gets to work on our order.

'I'm all by myself on a Friday night. Does that make me sad?'

'No, not at all. There's nothing wrong with enjoying your own company. I'm actually by myself too. I was supposed to be meeting a friend, but he cancelled.'

'I guess his loss is my gain.'

My new friend likes that answer, and as we receive our drinks, he formally introduces himself.

'Roger,' he tells me, offering me his hand.

'Fern,' I reply as I shake it, but as I do, he can't fail to notice the ring.

He doesn't say anything, but I can tell his demeanour has changed slightly and he's maybe worried that he's now wasting his time trying to chat up a taken woman.

'Oh, the ring thing. It's okay, I'm not married. Well, not anymore.'

'Oh, you're divorced?'

'Not exactly.'

I'm not sure if mentioning my fairly downbeat backstory is the best way of making bar talk on a Friday night, but as I don't want this guy to get the wrong idea, I decide to be honest.

'My husband passed away.'

'Oh, I'm so sorry.'

'It's okay. I'm getting there. Day by day.'

'I can't imagine. It must be so tough.'

'Yeah, it has been, especially with the way he died.'

Roger looks afraid to ask me to expand on that point, but I quite like how much sympathy this will get me from him, so I carry on.

'He was murdered.'

'What? Oh my God, that's awful. I'm so sorry. What

happened? No, wait, you don't have to answer that if you don't want to. We can talk about something else if you'd like.'

'It's okay, I like talking about him. It's important not to pretend it didn't happen.'

I take a moment to supposedly compose myself before I go on.

'He was having an affair and was killed by the other woman. I obviously didn't know about her until after it all happened.'

Roger looks horrified, and I bet he's asking himself why he chose to talk to me out of all the other women in this place.

'That's awful. I'm so sorry. What happened to the woman?'

'She's in prison now.'

'Good. Wow, that's crazy.'

'Yeah, they found the murder weapon on the beach with her fingerprints all over it. At least they caught her.'

'The beach?'

'Yeah, it happened up in Arberness.'

'Oh, wait, I remember hearing about that on the news. No way, you're the wife?'

'Yeah, unfortunately.'

Roger shakes his head, and I feel sorry for putting a dampener on his Friday night, so I try to give him a way out if he wants it.

'I'm sorry. You don't have to listen to me and my sob story. You're out to have fun. Don't feel bad if you want to go and talk to somebody else.'

'What? No, it's okay. Besides, I doubt I'm going to find anybody in here with a more interesting story than you, am I?'

His joke helps lifts the mood back to where it was before I started talking about death and infidelity, and as we move onto slightly less heavy topics, like the questionable behaviour of some of the people around us in this bar, I am wondering if it might be time to let a new man into my life. Nothing serious, of course, because I have to wait a little while longer to make it look like I'm still mourning Drew. But I can have a little fun, can't I? Lord knows I deserve it. And Lord knows it's been a while since a man I was interested in was interested in me too.

I'm reminded then of Rory, the last male to make a play for my affections, and after Roger has excused himself to visit the men's room, I take out my phone and type in his name. I instantly get several search results for Rory Richardson, and I click on the most recent news story, because I'm only interested in new developments where he is concerned.

This latest article talks about how a verdict of accidental death has been attributed to his case by a coroner, and that is what I was hoping for, so I allow myself a little smile before reading on. The article goes on to summarise how Rory's body was found, which was in the bathtub at his home, submerged beneath the water, and he was unresponsive to the medics who discovered him. The belief is that he passed out in the bathtub after drinking heavily and accidentally drowned, which is obviously tragic.

It's also not true.

I know that because I was there when Rory died. There was nothing accidental about it. After following him to his house after our conversation at the pub, I had led him to believe that I was willing to sleep with him in exchange for him staying quiet about what the two of us had done. But I'd realised back in that pub car park that if Rory was willing to blackmail me once then I would never truly be safe from him, no matter what I did. Add in the fact he had clearly developed a serious drinking problem, and he was such a liability that I had to do something.

Something as decisive as what I did to Drew and Alice.

After meeting Rory at his place, he had offered me a drink, which I declined, although that wasn't going to stop him partaking himself. Clearly wasted, he then made a pass at me, but I was able to fend him off by suggesting we go upstairs.

Giddy with excitement, he led me towards the bedroom, but it was as we were passing the bathroom that I suggested we have a little fun in there instead.

I told him a lie about how I liked to do it in the bath, and with his head filled with all sorts of images of my naked body beneath the soapy suds, he turned on the taps and allowed the water to fill up the tub.

Having instructed him to strip off, a command he couldn't comply with quickly enough, he then got into the bathtub while I sat behind him, massaging his shoulders and encouraging him to drink even more. It didn't take long for the alcohol and the hot water to work its magic, and as Rory got sleepy, I made sure to encourage him to sink even further down into the tub, easing his shoulders down until his head was barely above the water line.

When he fell asleep, I watched him slip under the water, and I was actually the one holding my breath as I waited for him to become starved of oxygen. I'm not sure exactly what I was expecting to happen because I'd never seen a person drown before. I had been hoping he would just stay under the water until he passed out, and then all I would have to do would be to leave. But Rory had suddenly woken up, and as his frightened eyes stared up at me from beneath the water, I knew he was only a second away from rising back up and gasping for air.

So that was why I put my hands on his chest and held him under.

He thrashed around a little, but his inebriated movements were weak, and I used gravity to my advantage, applying just enough downward force to prevent him from getting up but not enough to leave any marks on his skin that a police officer might have been interested in. The slick insides of the bathtub also helped me as Rory had nothing to grab onto to help him.

After several suffocating minutes, he stopped resisting. All that was left for me to do then was to wipe down a few of the surfaces in the bathroom, in case of any fingerprints, before I slipped out of his house and went back to my own, where I told my parents I was ready to leave after my head-clearing walk on the beach. Then we got into the car and drove away, leaving the village for good.

Mine and Drew's parents have been dealing with the sale of the house, meaning I haven't had to go back up there since, and I doubt I will ever return. That village and all that happened there certainly feels a million miles away from where I am right now, as I put my phone away and wait for Roger to come and re-join me at the bar.

When he does, he has a big grin on his face. When I ask why, he tells me it's because he has just requested a particular song to play. When it comes on, he insists that I dance to it with him. I've never been much of a dancer, but he does a good job of persuading me that I can change the habit of a lifetime. As the song begins to play, I leave my seat and follow him onto the dance floor.

As the pair of us get closer, his hands on my hips and our eyes only on each other and not the various other dancers surrounding us, I remember what it feels like to be wanted. Drew used to make me feel like this until he transferred that energy onto Alice instead. He paid the price for that, as did she. As for Rory, he was unfortunate, but he ultimately became collateral damage. Now, out of the four of us, I'm the one who has come out of all this the best, and as Roger twirls me around, I feel like things are looking up.

I might not be the doctor's wife anymore, but that's okay.

Who knows what might be next for me now this new man is in my life?

Bless him, Roger looks so happy as he shows me his moves and helps manoeuvre me around the floor. He's got a big grin on his face, like the cat who got the cream. He's thinking he's going to get lucky, and he just might. But of course, he's not that lucky, because he doesn't know who I really am, does he? He probably thinks I'm just some woman he can have a little fun with, but it'll be no big deal if things go sour between us, and he ends up leaving me a little less satisfied than I was before he met me.

Like I said, bless him. He doesn't have a clue, just like my ex-husband didn't either.

I'll just have to make sure I keep it that way.

And I'm sure I can.

After all, it's been this easy so far, right?

EPILOGUE

The man twirling Fern around the dance floor of the busy Manchester bar knew exactly what he was doing. He was being suave, sophisticated, funny and charming, and, most of all, he was displaying some neat moves as he moved to the music. All of it was being done with one thing in mind. To seduce his dance partner and hopefully get even closer to her than they were already now.

To anybody watching, it would have looked no different to the kind of thing that goes on in bars all over the world at this time of the week. Two strangers meeting, enjoying a few drinks and then getting even more acquainted as the inhibitions lower and the desire for human contact grows. But there was far more to this pair than met the eye. Fern, of course, had her own back-story, and what a story it was. But Roger was also somebody who had secrets, and despite the inner confidence of the woman he was dancing with, he was somebody who, for the first time ever, seemed to be one step ahead of her.

That was because Fern was not a stranger to him, and this chance meeting in a bar was not yet another random thing that the universe had allowed to transpire. Rather, it was a very deliberate act. Roger had followed Fern here, just like he had been following her for the past several days around this city, watching her eat, shop and enjoy her life. He had been following her, because he suspected there was more to her story than she was letting on.

Roger, or Greg as he was really called, had once been good friends with somebody who Fern had known well, though he had never crossed paths with the wife before. He had been friends with Drew, the late doctor, who had been a tennis-buddy of his, and the pair had shared the court many times over the years. Greg had chosen his pseudonym based on Drew's favourite tennis player, Roger Federer, aware that it would be less risky to get close to Fern by operating under an alias. But why the need for the deception?

It was because Greg felt Fern was hiding something.

After being dismayed to hear the news of Drew's death, Greg had found he didn't quite believe the idea that he had been killed by his mistress, because Drew had once confided in him about Alice. He knew how in love they were.

He felt there had to be more to it.

And he felt that Fern might hold the key to whatever that was.

It had all come about after Greg had recalled a conversation that he had had with Drew a few years before the doctor had left Manchester and moved to the village. It was there, after a game of tennis and several beers, that the subject of relationships and women had come up. Greg had joked about Drew being married and how he was unable to enjoy the single life anymore, before teasing him and suggesting he go and talk to a woman at the bar. It was just boyish, banal banter, but Drew's reply to that challenge had always stuck with Greg.

'Do you have any idea what my wife would do to me if she thought I was trying it on with other women?' he'd said, aghast but honestly. 'She'd kill me, I have no doubt about that.'

Greg had thought his friend was joking, but Drew had then mentioned a time when he had rather foolishly been messaging a woman he used to go to medical school with, and even though the messages were purely platonic, Fern had found out about them. When she had, she had almost thrown his phone against the wall, called him a cheat and got so angry that he thought she was going to hit him. He had managed to calm her down in the end and persuade her that nothing was going on, which was true, but it had been a rather eye-opening insight into how his wife could behave if she thought she was being cheated on.

That was why, after the news of Drew's murder and the revelation that he had been having an affair, Greg had thought about Fern and how she would have reacted if she had known about it, which apparently she didn't. But when Alice was sentenced for the crime, Greg wondered if perhaps it was all a little too neat a story. He wondered if, somehow, Fern had known about the affair beforehand, and if she had, she sure had figured out a brilliant way to get revenge. But that was just a wild idea at that point, and one he wasn't confident to voice with anybody. That was until he read about the death of a Rory Richardson, the partner of Alice, the woman who was in prison for Drew's murder.

The reports said Rory had got drunk and fallen asleep in his bathtub, and plenty of people in the village had added weight to the reports, saying how they had seen Rory drinking heavily after his wife's sentencing and, in particular, at the pub the day he was believed to have died. But what was his reason for being at the pub that day?

Fern's leaving party.

Greg couldn't help but think it was a hell of a coincidence that something bad would happen to Rory on Fern's last day in the village, considering how they were already connected thanks to what their respective partners had done together. After giving it some thought, he came to the belief that Fern and

Rory had taken revenge on their cheating spouses but that, for some reason, before she left the village Fern had decided to tie up the loose end and silence the only person who knew what she had done.

It was a line of thinking that came quite easy to a man like Greg, who had spent several years as a police officer in his twenties and early thirties before leaving the force to seek out a more favourable work/life balance. Having been trained to be sceptical and not take everything at face value, he had become adept at seeing all the possibilities in a case and not just what the obvious evidence pointed to. In fact, he was quite surprised the detective in charge of Drew's murder investigation had not felt the same way, but perhaps he had and maybe it was the internal politics of the police force that had dampened his enthusiasm there. Greg knew all about that side of the job too, which was another reason he had been eager to get out and do something else with his life.

The theory that Greg had landed on might have all sounded very far-fetched, but he had been unable to sleep once he had the idea in his mind and, despite it being a hell of a long shot, he had plucked up the courage to take his suspicions to a few of his old colleagues in the police, presuming they would look into it because, at best, it was their job to do so, and, at worst, they might do him the favour for old time's sake.

Despite their former relationship with him, they had not been interested because, as far as they were concerned, the culprit in Drew's murder was already behind bars, so the case was closed, and Fern's story was airtight. Rory's death was ruled accidental, so there was nothing to look into there. But Greg wasn't prepared to let it go, remembering just how nervous his friend had been when he talked about Fern and her reaction to those messages. From other conversations he'd had with his friend Drew, he knew Fern had a different side to her, a side capable of overreaction and intense anger. It was a side that no one else seemed to see, because all she showed in public was that of being the loyal and loving doctor's wife. That was why he wasn't ready to let things lie, and if the police weren't going to investigate her, he would have to do it himself.

So that was his plan. He was going to befriend her and then, as he got closer, try to find out if she really was capable of what he thought she had done. It was risky, because if he was right then he was dealing with somebody capable of committing and covering up very serious crimes, but he felt he owed it to Drew and, of course, Alice, who he had never met but had admired from afar, after seeing photos of her both online and in the recent news coverage, and who he feared might be serving a sentence for a crime she didn't commit.

He had even gone so far as to write a letter to Alice while she served her sentence behind bars, under yet another pseudonym, of course, in which he expressed his belief that she was innocent and incapable of such a heinous crime. Alice had actually written back and, while parts of the letter had clearly been redacted by the prison authorities, he was able to get the gist of what Alice was saying.

She was innocent.

She just couldn't figure out how she had been made to look guilty.

But Greg felt he knew, and it was now time to start proving it.

He might not admit it, but he had perhaps fallen a little under Alice's spell in the time since, just like his late friend had, as more letters were exchanged between the pair. But he wasn't pursuing his plan purely out of romantic reasons. He wanted justice for his old friend and, overall, justice for the families of the deceased.

As Fern danced beside the man she thought would never know her secrets, he danced beside the woman who did not know his. He was going to get even closer to her and hopefully start a relationship with her. As time went by, he would be watching and waiting for one little mistake. One slip-up. One thread that Fern had failed to tie up and one that he could unravel until he had the evidence to expose the whole thing. It might be a text message somewhere. It might be a diary entry. It might even be a slip of the tongue during a conversation in bed one day, a conversation that Greg would be secretly recording on his phone, because he was going to do all he could to have a record of her words and movements over the coming weeks and months.

Only time would tell if he was successful in catching her out, and be able to do what no one else had done.

Only time would tell if he would be the one to reveal the true nature of the pleasant, pretty and seemingly perfect doctor's wife.

A LETTER FROM DANIEL

Dear reader,

I want to say a huge thank you for choosing to read *The Doctor's Wife*. If you did enjoy it and would like to keep up to date with all my latest releases, please sign up at the following link. Your email address will never be shared and you can unsubscribe at any time.

www.bookouture.com/daniel-hurst

I hope you loved *The Doctor's Wife* and, if you did, I would be very grateful if you could write an honest review. I'd love to hear what you think, and it makes such a difference in helping new readers to discover my books for the first time.

I love hearing from my readers, and you can get in touch with me directly at my email address daniel@danielhurstbooks.com. I reply to every message! You can also visit my website where you can download a free psychological thriller called *Just One Second*.

Thank you,

Daniel

KEEP IN TOUCH WITH DANIEL

www.danielhurstbooks.com

facebook.com/danielhurstbooks
instagram.com/danielhurstbooks

CPSIA information can be obtained
at www.ICGtesting.com
Printed in the USA
LVHW091318240723
753250LV00003B/347